Laurence James Nicolson

Songs of Thule

Laurence James Nicolson

Songs of Thule

ISBN/EAN: 9783744769082

Printed in Europe, USA, Canada, Australia, Japan

Cover: Foto ©Andreas Hilbeck / pixelio.de

More available books at **www.hansebooks.com**

He dreamt he saw his northern skies,
His pining heart grew strong,
And with glad tears within his eyes,
He wakened into song.

CONTENTS.

Contents.

8 *Contents.*

SONGS OF THULE.

"THE BARD OF THULE."

HE dreamt he saw his north'rn skies,
　His pining heart grew strong,
And with glad tears within his eyes,
　He wakened into song.

He sang of " merry dancers " light,
　That showed where lay in foam,
Like silver clasping jewels bright,
　The isles he called his home.

Of crags uniting sea and sky,
　Green isles and lonely caves,
The sea-bird's cry, the wind's reply,
　And roar of ocean waves.

I

The organ tone of temples vast
　　Uprising from the deep ;
A mem'ry dwells in every blast
　　That through their arches sweep.

He roamed, a boy, the heather hills,
　　He wandered by the shore,
And then awoke in joyous thrills
　　The love his young heart bore.

And growing, strength'ning with his years,
　　First love his loves among,
With light of smiles, and rain of tears,
　　It blossomed into song.

The sobbing of the troubled sea,
　　The restless night wind's moan,
Found in his soul a harmony,
　　That sorrow made her own.

The eagle in his fearless flight
　　With freedom-loving wing ;
The gentle light of north'rn night,
　　Of these he loved to sing.

His love was deep, his hate was strong,
  And side by side they ran ;
One music making in his song
  The brotherhood of man.

One eve, on city, spire, and dome,
  Light fell he could not see ;
At last ! at last ! 'mid scenes of home
  In fevered dream was he.

Came voices, as he sank in sleep,
  From islands far away ;
He smiled—and on the shoreless deep
  The bard of Thule lay.

Oh where have you wandered to, under what sky !
I see the old schoolhouse, now lonely and still,
I see the rough road winding up the steep hill,
The long stretch of sand, where in childhood we played;
But the years come between, and the glory has fled,—
Ah ! the years come between, and the glory has fled.

> Only in dreams do thy headlands appear ;
> Only in dreams are the voices I hear ;
> Joy of my heart ! all the dearer to me,
> Thule, my fatherland ! over the sea.

I stand on the cliff, looking out to the sea,
The breeze blowing inland is whispering to me ;
Wherever by fortune the exile may roam
The sea-breeze ! the sea-breeze will waft his heart
     home,—
Will joyfully welcome the wanderer home.
Though severed from thee, yet united we stand,
And circling around, and with hand grasping hand,
The pledge of each true-hearted Norseman shall be,
The islands that rest on the far northern sea,—
The grand rugged isles of the far northern sea.

Bearded lips quiver, ne'er quivered before;
Eyes that were tearless, are now brimming o'er;
So the fond heart offers homage to thee,
Thule, my fatherland ! Queen of the sea.

THE ISLES OF THULE.

Tune, — " Killarney."

WHERE the " merry dancers " bright
  Flit along the northern sky ;
Basking in their fairy light,
  Thule's bays and islands lie.
Boldly tower her crags on high,
  And the sounding ocean waves,
Mingling with the sea-bird's cry,
  Echo through her lonely caves.
        Dreamlike o'er the senses come,
        Mem'ries dear of love and home ;
        Every wavelet's rippling flow
        Murmurs sweet of long ago.

Dancing gaily on the wave,
  Or mid' storm and seething foam,
What will not the fisher brave ·
  For the dear ones left at home ?

Watching as the storm comes on—
　　Ah ! how many there may mourn,
When the weary watch is done,
　　Friends who never will return !
　　　　Dreamlike o'er the senses come,
　　　　Mem'ries dear of love and home ;
　　　　Whisp'ring waves, or storm's loud roar,
　　　　All recall that dear lov'd shore.

Where the " merry dancers " bright
　　Flit along the northern skies :—
When life's twilight shades to-night,
　　Let me close my fading eyes ;
Hearing still the sea-bird's cry,
　　As in childhood long ago,
Mingling in wild harmony
　　With the sounding waves below—
　　　　Waves that were my playmates wild
　　　　When on Thule's shores a child ;
　　　　Into slumber long and deep,
　　　　Hush me at the last to sleep.

THE NORSEMAN'S BATTLE SONG.

LIGHT is breaking on the shore,
Norsemen bend the flashing oar ;
Onward on the roaring wind,
Kith and kin we leave behind.
   Round the headland towering o'er us,
   Do the deed that lies before us,
   Worthy of the land that bore us :
Should the darkness fill mine eyes,
I shall die as Viking dies ;
Find me when the fight is done,
Where the gods might claim a son,
      Bear me home,
      O'er the foam,
    In the battle gear,
    My good ship my bier ;
  Let the fire arise and flame the day.
      Seaward gale,
      Swell the sail,

Till the deep afar,

Shines a mighty star,

And right royally I pass away ;

When Valhalla's walls shall ring

Welcome to the warrior king.

Norsemen sweep upon the foe,

Battle-axe, and brand, and bow,

Sweep as when, with ocean roar,

Tempests sweep along the shore ;

Scalds shall sing the saga hoary,

Hearts be kindled by the story,

Brave old Norseland reap the glory.

Victory ! he cried, and fell,

But his troth he kept full well—

Dead, on dead, at close of day,

There the grim old Viking lay.

Bear him home,

O'er the foam,

In the battle gear,

His good ship his bier ;

Let the fire arise and flame the day,

Seaward gale,

Swell the sail,

Till the deep afar,

Shines a mighty star,

And right royally he'll pass away,

Then Valhalla's walls shall ring

Welcome to the warrior king.

THULE.

BELOVED Thule, I am thine !
  Thy home is on the northern deep,
Embosomed there, thou art so fair,
  The summer day is robbed of sleep,
And love-lorn night, a lonely star,
Can but behold thee from afar.

Can but behold thee from afar,
  And whisper : " Heart, oh heart, be still,"
For jealous day will not away,
  But lingers on from hill to hill,
And oh, the light on land and sea,
A dream, a deathless memory.

A dream, a deathless memory,
  That gathers glory more and more,
Where headlands rise to cloudless skies,
  With ceaseless song of sea and shore ;
Beloved Thule, I am thine !
And thou, first love and last, art mine.

COMFORT.

Can there be comfort and strife
  Raging within like the sea ?
Give me my dead back to life,
  Then speak of comfort to me.

Have I not prayed all the night ?
  Is He not mighty to save ?
What answer brought morning light ?
  Ask of the merciless wave.

Ah, you may call it a sin.
  Mine is the anguish to-day ;
Where—for the darkness within—
  Where is the light can you say ?

There as he stood at the door,
  Light of my soul in his eyes ;
Never again !—nevermore !—
  Come ye and see where he lies.

Eyes needing no more the light,
  Ears heeding no more the din ;
Joy once to hearing and sight,
  Let ye his little ones in.

Little eyes—what do they see ?
  Little tongues—what do they say ?
Hushed is their boisterous glee,
  Father is sleeping to-day.

One creeps up close to the dead,
  Kisses the cheek tenderly ;
One lifts a bright curly head,
  Mother ! wake father to me.

Back with a look of surprise
  Come they, and cling to her dress ;
Motherly love fills her eyes ;
  Breaks from her lips—" Fatherless ! "

Ah me ! the long dreary night ;
  Ah me ! the long weary years ;
Darlings—oh clasp—clasp me tight—
  Is there not comfort in tears ?

A LULLABY.

Hushyba, my curry ting,
   Cuddle close to mammie ;
Cuddle close and hear me sing,
   Peerie mootie lammie.
Glancin' goold and siller shells
   Fae da mermaid's dwellin',
Bonnie flo'ers fae fairy dells,
   Past a' mortal tellin' ;
Wha, oh wha sall get but de,
Hert o' my hert, life o' me.

Saftly, saftly, hümin grey
   Owre de sea is creepin',
An' its nedder nicht nor day,
   Waking time, nor sleepin' ;
But da waves upo' da shore
   Whisper still my lammie,

Doun da lum, an' troo da door ;
  Cuddle close to mammie.
Cosier du couldna be—
Hert o' my hert, life o' me.

Bonnie blue een blinkin' fast,
  Peerie mootie lammie ;
Sleep has ta'en de noo at last,
  Cuddlin' close to mammie.
Blissens be attendin' de,
  Happy be dy wakin',
For wir ain comes fae da sea,
  Whin da day is breakin'.
Daybreak, licht o' hame is he—
Hert o' my hert, life o' me.

NOTE.—Curry—Neat, bonnie, lovable, are included in this comprehensive word, and do not exhaust its meaning. Perrie mootie
—very small ; ting—thing ; fae—from ; nedder—neither ; da—
the ; du—thou ; dy—thy ; upo—upon ; troo—through ; de—thee ;
blissens—blessings ; wir—our ; hümin—twilight.

BARBARA PITCAIRN.

A NORLAN' BALLAD.

" 'Tis said wi' young Gifford in secret ye meet,
    Noo, mark ye my words, if the story be true ;
I'd rather my son were stretched dead at my feet,
    Barbara Pitcairn, than wedded to you."

The lady o' Büsta was stately an' grand,
    An' prood was my lady o' her pedigree ;
But Barbara Pitcairn only dwelt on the land,
    And savin' her bonnie face, naething had she.

The wavelets fell saft on the silvery sand
    As doun through the valley she wearily gaed ;
The singin' o' birdies rang blythe o'er the land,
    But she never heard the sweet music they made.

The bairnies at play missed the licht o' her smile,
    The flowers raised their heads, for they croon'd her
        their queen ;

2

The glory o' sunshine fell round her the while,
    But she naething saw but her sorrow sae keen.

" Is this my ain dearest wi' tears in her een—
    Her bonnie face white as the new-driven snaw ?
Oh, whaur hae ye been, love, an' what hae ye seen ?
    An' why keep ye turnin' your sweet face awa' ? "

" I've been at the ha', an' my lady is there,
    An' oh, sic a fear has ta'en haud o' me a' !
My heart is fu' sair—I can tell ye na mair ;
    An', oh, that ye werena the laird o' the ha'.

" I'm wae for yoursel' an' what yet may befa',
    I'm wae—oh, I'm wae for the bairnie unborn ;
Sae weel may my face be as white as the snaw,
    For surely o' women am I maist forlorn."

Sae closely he faulded her into his airms,
    An' kissed her fu' aft and fu' tenderly ;
" Oh, wha could hae heart ane sae gentle to harm,
    Or bring ony dule 'tween my ain love and me ?

" We plighted our troth we would ever be true,
    We plighted our troth, an' we sealed it for life ;
  The secret is oot noo, but think ye I rue
    The day before God that I made ye my wife ?

" This night for the proof I will cross owre the voe ;
    Nae rest will I seek till I get it, my queen !
  An' then to the ha' wi' my darlin' I'll go,
    To-morrow ! to-morrow ! the proof shall be seen ! "

" Oh, Gifford, my ain love, I ken ye are true ;
    What care I for wealth, or a lady to be ?
  Your smile is my sunshine, I bask in it noo,
    If that were ta'en frae me I think I wad dee."

Like maiden sae pensive the northern night
    Cam' doon owre the land as the day closed his e'e ;
  The moon has arisen, an' what meets her sight ?
    A masterless boat driftin' oot to the sea.

Sweet sleep has fu' tenderly smoothed every broo,
    The hillside abune, an' the valley below ;
  But sleep—deeper sleep—has encompassed him noo,
    Whase bed is the wanderin' wave o' the voe.

The skerries are singin' his dirge in the dawn,
   The cry o' the sea-bird is lanely and wae;
One star in the wide heaven, sickly and wan,
   Is fadin' awa' frae the light o' the day.

The light on his eyes, yet in darkness he lies,
   He lies on the sand that the bright waters lave;
An' aye the refrain comes again and again,
   The cry o' the sea bird, the plash o' the wave.

But she—wha is she at the low cottage door?—
   The spirit o' mornin'—the sunlight her hair;
A moment she stands wi' her een on the shore,
   An' noo wi' quick feet she is there—she is there.

"Oh, Gifford!" she cries—as she sinks on the sand,
   And looks on the white face, wet, wet, frae the sea,
An' kissin' the cauld lips, an' grippin' the hand—
   "Oh, Gifford! my Gifford! speak! oh, speak to me!

"Ye ask—wha am I, wi' sic grief for the dead:
   Oh, lady, the answer ye've ta'en frae his breast;
My love, an' my life noo, to sorrow are wed—
   Ye've ta'en frae his breast what will tell ye the rest.

" Aye, there is the proof—next his heart it was worn!
    Aye, there is the proof, an' it cost him his life!
But saves noo frae slander his bairnie unborn,
    An' me, noo his widow, for I was his wife."

They stand face to face, an' their tearfu' een meet,
    A voice like an echo thrills baith their hearts through;
" I'd rather my son was stretched dead at my feet,
    Barbara Pitcairn, than wedded to you."

THULE NO MORE.

A SONG OF LEAVE-TAKING.

Tune—"The Hardy Norseman."

FAREWELL to rocky hill and glen,
  Green isles and deep-voic'd shore,
The stranger may return again,
  But we return no more.
For gather'd now upon thy shore,
  An exile band are we,
And nevermore, oh, nevermore,
  Our eyes may light on thee.

Our limbs are strong, our hearts are brave,
  Nurs'd by the wild North Sea ;
A home we seek across the wave,
  Dear Thule, far from thee.
But still, as in the days of yore,
  Thy children still are we,

Though nevermore, oh, nevermore
 Our eyes may light on thee.

Thy tow'ring cliffs majestic rise
 From ocean depth below,
And grander anthems fill thy skies
 Than human temples know.
And in the vanish'd days of yore
 We listen'd reverently,
Now nevermore, oh, nevermore
 Our eyes may light on thee.

We see thee yet, dear island home,
 And strain our tear-dimm'd sight
Across an angry sea of foam,
 Through gath'ring clouds of night.
Farewell, farewell, thy fading shore
 Sinks in the North'rn Sea,
And nevermore, oh, nevermore
 Our eyes may light on thee.

THE PRINCESS OF THULE.

WITHIN the mighty city pining lay
The fair young princess at the close of day;
The glory in the west had lingered long,
And touched the chords of memory and song.

Oh fain would I flee from the strife and the din,
Where hearts that were pure know the glamour of sin,
And rough-shod men go where the roses are spread,
But bare are the feet that the thorny way tread,
   And weary the hearts for the hopes that are dead.
I see the lone land of the mist and the fell,
The purple-clad vales where mine own people dwell,
I hear their dear voices now calling to me—
Oh, Thule, dear Thule! my heart is with thee ;
   Oh, Thule, my island home over the sea.
      Oh can it be but a dream of the night,
      Filling and thrilling my heart with delight,
      Only to fade when the morning shall rise ;
      Then let me die with the dream in mine eyes.

There! there! the grim headlands of Thule arise,
Her walls to the waves, and her cliffs to the skies:
And oh, her wild music is dear unto me,
The cry of the seabird, the surge of the sea,
   The sound of the great throbbing northern sea.
The days that are gone, with the rapture of soul,
Return on the winds with the billowy roll;
And shall I not have a glad welcome from thee,
Oh, Thule, dear island home over the sea!
   Oh, Thule, my Thule, I come back to thee!
     Oh can it be but a dream of the night,
     Filling and thrilling my heart with delight,
     Only to fade when the morning shall rise;
     Then let me die with the dream in mine eyes.

LERWICK.

OLD AND NEW.

TO-DAY we long for yesterday,
  Ah, Time, that flies so fast!
A gentle breeze of memories
  Is stirring up the past.

In mystic gleam of vision clear,
  I see the haunts of yore,
There's Sinclair's beach and Gallie's pier,
  And Marion Mouat's shore.

And Morrison's and Parker's piers,
  And Burns's, Tait's, and Hay's;
Before my sight they rise in light—
  " The light of other days."

Loadberrys * lie like anchored ships,
  And they are anchored well;
Ah, if their oaken doors were lips,
  What stories they could tell!

Can I forget your slimy steps,
  Greig's "hol," of evil fame?
Once, ere I wist, on your death list,
  You nearly had my name.

At last, at last! oh dear old town,
  I journey back to thee,
Across the foam—for there is home—
  And now what do I see?

I walk, where once I rowed a boat,
  A stranger and alone;
And see with eyes of sad surprise
  That everything is gone.

Yea, everything I knew thee by;
  Now what art thou to me?

---

* Cellars' or stores built on the shore, nearly surrounded by the
sea.

An old-world gleam—a bye-gone dream,
    A sacred memory.

For thou art dead, old Lerwick town,
    And never more will rise ;
It had to be—ah, yes—but we
    Look back with loving eyes.

" The king is dead !—long live the king!"
    And cheer the progress made.
And yet—and yet—can we forget
    The dear old king that's dead ?

THE DARK AND THE FAIR.

ONE rose before my raptured eyes,
   Like Norlan' summer night,
One floated down from Indian skies,
   With eyes of melting light ;
And both—ah, me ! do what I may,
Possess my being night and day.

When she—the dark one—takes my hand,
   And gazes in my eyes,
My soul is wafted to that land,
   The lover's paradise ;
Then she—the fair one—whispers low,
And where she leads me I must go.

Oh ! maiden of the Norlan' seas,
   My dream—divinely fair ;
I envy e'en the passing breeze
   That wantons through thy hair ;

But what avails ?—with killing art
The dark eyes stab me to the heart.

How can I choose in my despair,
   The dark eyes, or the blue?
Beloved angels !—tell me where
   Is land between the two ;
For I am on a shoreless sea,
Four star-bright eyes distracting me.

BALTA.*

In tempest or in calm, by day or night,
   Round Thule's shores do no fond mem'ries dwell?
Great Saxafiord, the last that filled your sight,
   And Baltasound, birth-haven loved so well.

You sent a kindly greeting unto me,
   A hope that we should meet some happy day,
But, ere the season neared when it should be,
   A message came that you had passed away.

Sweet singer on the battle-field of life,
   Soul tuned to love of right and hate of wrong,
Brave heart, that waged a hopeless double strife,
   We hear again your simple Doric song—

     " For, 'midst the difficulty great
       Wi' whilk I hae to cope,

---

* The *nom-de-plume* of a young poet whom Death hath taken.

There's aye a light shines unco bright,
 What can it be but hope ? .
An' surely some bright day will come,
 I kenna when or hoo,
When I can cry triumphantly,
 ' It's my turn noo.' " ·

The last, the last you sung in that strong light,
 The mystic light that ever led you on,
Then all too soon came down the silent night ;
 Oh, was the light the sunset or the dawn ?

It was the dawn ! it was the dawn that came,
 And so at last you did not sing in vain ;
For Death came near, and called upon your name,
 And doubly true became your song's refrain.

And now with one who never saw your face,
 Nor felt the kindly touch of hand to hand,
A brotherhood is sealed with nameless grace,
 And consecrated in the silent land.

THE CAPTAIN AND HIS MATE.

Set to Music by A. STEWART.

A SONG, a wedding song to-night,
　A golden wedding song;
Old eyes still bright, by love's own light,
　And two hearts brave and strong.
　　The captain and his mate,
　　　Thro' calm and stormy weather,
　　By love's decree have sailed life's sea
　　　For fifty years together.

They hear the wedding bells again,
　From out the long ago;
And welcome sunshine, welcome rain,
　And now the winter snow.
　　And now the winter snow,
　　　For love, the darkest weather
　　Will battle through, when hearts are true,
　　　For fifty years together.

3

The day is rife of toil and strife,
 But evening bringeth rest ;
The light we trace on either face,
 Is light from out the west.
  But stronger, brighter still,
   Through calm and stormy weather,
  The light that lies in loving eyes
   For fifty years together.

With hearty cheer, safe harboured here,
 And love on either side ;
Tight fore and aft, long may their craft
 In peaceful waters ride.
  And till the night shall come,
   With dark and dreary weather,
  The love will last that stood the blast
   For fifty years together.

"STAND BY THE FORE-SHEET." *

THE love of comrades comes with balmy breath
    Across the sea of death,
And sweetens sorrow for the young and brave,
    That found one grave.

"Stand by the fore-sheet!" and one stood and fell,
    The sea—he loved so well—
With jealous heart, in her white arms of foam,
    Then bore him home.

His comrade, in his eager haste to save,
    Plunged headlong in the wave;
In vain, in vain, they went down side by side
    Beneath the tide.

---

* The above verses refer to the unfortunate accident whereby two gentlemen lost their lives on the Shetland coast. One was about to be married—the wedding cards having been issued.

A maiden waits in fair Edina's town
  For one, her life to crown ;
And counts the hours that keep him still apart
  From her glad heart.

Oh never shall that maiden's arms enfold
  Her lover stark and cold ;
And dark to her will be for evermore
  Lone Thule's shore.

But dearer now the ever-present past,
  The first kiss and the last ;
And in her heart the wild wave sinks and swells,
  With wedding bells.

The bride and bridegroom now, in very truth,
  Have gained immortal youth ;
The favoured guests full well may hold for aye
  The wedding day.

KATE.

FAREWELL! sweet one, that I adore,
   My heart, my heart is thine most truly,
Thy face will haunt me evermore,
   My own belovéd maid of Thule.

We part—but for a little space,
   All, all thou art, now know I fully,
How, how can I forget thy face!
   My own belovéd maid of Thule.

What though I leave the happy shore,
   Ah, wind and wave, that part us cruelly,
Thy face will haunt me evermore,
   My own belovéd maid of Thule.

My song I dedicate to thee—
   And I would dedicate a dozen—
But fate will sever thee and me,
   For I am forty, and thy cousin;

Yet I, I will forget thee not:

What though our love has thus miscarried,

And now—I almost had forgot

Another item—I am married!

THE HYLTA DANCE.*

A NORTHERN LEGEND.

THE Hylta Dance, my little one,
  Is just a fairy ring;
When all is still about the hill,
  The fairies dance and sing.

They dance and sing in merry ring
  Around their fiddlers three;
And all the night, in wild delight,
  Are free, as free can be.

We wander on—my boy and I,
  All under that sweet spell,
With little speech, until we reach
  The middle of the dell.

---

* The name given to a ring of stones, with three in the centre,
embedded in the green sward in the island of Fetlar, Shetland.

The lonely hills on either side,
　　Near by—the restless sea ;
A ring of stones outspreading wide,
　　And in the centre, three.

Here is the fairy ring, my child,
　　"Where are the fairies gone?"
They must away, ere dawn of day,
　　For night is theirs alone.

But some, alas ! had lingered late ;
　　In vain they made their moan,
The sun arose, their life blood froze,
　　And they were changed to stone.

So in a circle here they stand,
　　Just as they stood that day ;
Now round the ring, all hand in hand,
　　The merry children play.

It is an old, old story, child,
　　That poets oft have sung,
Long, long ago, for you must know
　　The world then was young.

With wonderment he takes my hand,
   I leave the ways of men :
Oh, gentle power ! for one brief hour
   I am a boy again.

It is not day—it is not night,*
   But hill, and dell, and stream,
In Norlan' light, before my sight,
   Arise—a rapture dream.

The whisper of the homeless wind,
   The sound of sea and shore,
Bring back the past from out the vast,
   My own for evermore.

With ears—the master Time makes keen,
   With eyes, that look through tears—
All tenderly, I hear and see
   The ghosts of bygone years.

A child among the children I,
   I hear them laugh and sing,

---

* The light that remains in a Shetland midsummer sky after the
sun has set has to be seen to be for ever remembered.

And, hand in hand, I join the band
   Around the fairy ring.

Bright, living fairies long ago,
   "Where are the fairies gone?"
My little boy, I do not know,
   For I am here alone.

A SUMMER DAY.

WE met by the shores of the Forth,
  From islands far over the sea,
Whose headlands arise in the North,
  Storm-daring, defiant, and free.
We thought of our home-land afar,
  As wave followed wave on the shore.
Oh ! well-beloved Northern Star,
  We are thine ! we are thine evermore !

Our Norlan' tongue, gifted by thee,
  Fell soft on our ear where we met,
And wafted from over the sea
  The song we can never forget.
It came with the bird on the wing,
  It came with the wave on the shore,
And ever again our refrain
  We are thine ! we are thine evermore !

We gathered ourselves in a ring :
   With song, and with dance, and with play,
Our city-freed spirits took wing
   To childhood and home far away ;
And though beneath alien sky,
   That one day will ever recall
The home-light that never will die
   Till death overshadoweth all.

DA BREADWINNER.

Oʜ, midder, I ken for yer face is sae white,
  I ken bi da tears in yer ee,
Yer thinkin' agen o' my faeder, da nicht
  'At he gaed awa' ta da sea.

What laek wis my faedar? tell a' 'at ye can,
  Did ever I sit on his knee?
Dy faedar, my bairn? A kindlier man
  Never pat oot a boat ta da sea.

But, midder, if he kens yer greetin' sae sair,
  Wid he no come hame frae da sea?
Oh, na, na, my jewel, his een never mair
  Will licht on his bairn or me.

Come sit on my knee, an' I'll tell a' I ken,
  Noo cuddle in close, close ta me ;
Dy faeder, my bairn wi' five ither men,
  At hümin set oot ta da sea.

He stood here an' kïssed dee an' me, ere he gaed ;
   Cam' back frae da door aince agen,
An' kissed dee, my darlin', looked at me, an' said,
   " Güdewife—a last kiss ta oor ain."

I cam' ta da door, bit I spak no a wird,
   I felt as if a' wisna richt ;
I stood till his boat just looked like a bird,
   I stood, till she gaed frae my sicht.

'Tween sleepin' an' wakin', I couldna tell hoo,
   I toucht dat dy faedar wis here,
An' twice I cried—" Willie ! " but den, my ain doo,
   My mind wis dementit wi' faer.

Doo's sleepin', my bairn ; oh, sweet be dy sleep,
   For trouble enough doo may dree,
Dy hert is owre young for da sorrow sae deep
   Dat bears doon sae heavy on me.

But paice efter tempest will come yet, I ken,
   Laek saft moonlicht owre da still sea,
Sae gladly I'll welcome da nichtfa, for den
   At daybreak da shadows will flee.

BALDER THE BEAUTIFUL.

FAR in the Northland, 'mid seething sea foam
Where the bold Norseman has found him a home;
Round the grim headlands defiant and lone,
Down through the sea caves with sob and with moan
  Sea-bird above and the wild wave below
  Echo and answer with voices of woe—
     Balder the Beautiful!
     Balder is dead.

Laid in his ship with his face to the skies,
Crowned with his golden hair let the flame rise;
Wind and wave waft him to ocean afar,
Lonely and grand till he fades to a star.
  Sea-bird above and the wild wave below
  Answer and echo with voices of woe—
     Balder the Beautiful!
     Balder is dead.

Gone are the gods in the twilight of days,
Gone with the hearts that accorded them praise ;
Yet do they reign, and when spring breezes blow,
Waking the earth into blossom, we know,
   Out of the Northland and over the sea,
   Filled with the hope of the joy that shall be,
      Balder the Beautiful !
      Cometh again.

Mighty the deeds that the Sagamen sing,
Done in the days when the earth was in spring ;
Now, in full summer, what breezes will blow,
Waking the heart into blossom, and show.
   Out of the Northland and over the sea,
   Filled with the hope of the day that shall be,
      Balder the Beautiful !
      Coming again.

"DU KENS MY HERT IS DINE."

" Du kens my hert is dine,"
    Was all that she could say ;
And in the bliss of one long kiss
    We parted on that day.
A wanderer was I,
    At fickle Fortune's call ;
The roaring sea was joy to me,
    For love was all in all.

The golden sun her hair,
    The foam her bosom white ;
Her deep-blue eyes the Norlan' skies
    On cloudless summer night.
The music of her voice
    No bard has ever sung ;
For bird and breeze and sounding seas
  · Are in her Norlan' tongue.

4

Oh, love is all in all,
　My hope, my guiding light
Go where I may, my sun by day,
　My star in darkest night.
In tempest or in calm
　One dream is mine alway;
To cross again the heaving main
　To Norlan' far away.

With years of golden gain
　I now seek Thule's shore;
All danger past, to thee at last,
　My own for evermore.
Oh, whither shall I go?
　What comfort now is mine?
Above her grave I murmur low,
　"Du kens my hert is dine."

OUR FATHERLAND.

My friend! to me not all in vain,
  The ling'ring days have circled round,
For I shall cross the northern main,   •
  And walk once more on sacred ground.

New friends are but the passing breath,
  That gently stirs a summer sea,
Old friends are linked by solemn Death,
  And live—on loving memory.

Again with thrill of glad surprise,
  Upon the deck I see you stand,
And meet the welcome of your eyes,
  And grasp again your manly hand.

Grand Saxafiord, and Hermaness,
  Arise before our raptured sight,
And Cliff in utter loneliness,
  And over all, the northern night.

Oh did I say—"the northern night?"
  There is no night on Thule's shore,
Enamoured Day leaves ling'ring light,
  That haunts the soul for evermore.

By lovely Loch of Cliff—we stand ;
  Oh noble hills on either side !
Could you not stay the ruthless hand
  That spread destruction far and wide !

He saw the happy peasant's home,
  And envy filled his greedy mind ;
Afar the homeless exiles roam,
  And roofless cots are left behind.

The little households wandered forth,
  And hearts might break, and tears be shed ;
The stranger sought the stormy north
  The stranger ate the children's bread.

Our joyous thoughts were touched with pain,
  With full hearts joined we hand to hand,
And reverently—we pledged to thee,
  Our Fatherland !—Our Fatherland !

"THE SEA HATH SPOKEN."

(Isaiah xxiii. 4.)

The sea hath spoken,
Even the mighty and merciless sea,
And hearts are broken,
Where is there comfort, if comfort there be?

Swift without warning,
Burst forth the tempest in death-dealing might,
Oh God for morning!
Cry of the helpless that terrible night.

Skilful and daring,
Aye, but the darkness came down like a pall,
Then came despairing,
When the death agony swept over all.

Thule, Oh Thule!
What though thy waves dimple now into smiles,

The Sea Hath Spoken.

Know we not truly,
Sorrow is queen of thy cliff-girted isles.

The sea hath spoken,
What is the answer brought back from the shore?
This shall betoken,
All the air echoes the sad "nevermore."

Tireless, Oh tireless,
Wail of the widow—the widow new made;
And from homes fireless,
Cometh the cry of the orphan for bread.

LAURENCE MOAR.

A son of Thule, gentle, true, and brave,
  He fought the wild North wave :
Brought home the dead and dying through the fight,
  That direful night.

A peacefu' sea lapped cliff and shore when he,
  And his companions three,
For wife and little ones, set out, and found
  Their fishing ground.

Upon them like a Fury, fierce and fast,
  Drove down the bitter blast,
And tore in wrath, with desolating sweep,
  The mighty deep.

They cut their lines, and each man took his oar,
  And laboured for the shore,
But their small craft, though handled manfully,
  Swept out to sea.

The stinging snow like fine dust choked their breath,
    They fought Despair and Death ;
The wave broke over them, the tempest rose,
    Their life blood froze,

The deadly darkness, leagued with wind and wave,
    Closed o'er them like a grave,
And by the touch alone each brave man knew
    His comrade true.

But shoulder still to shoulder, blow for blow,
    They felt and fought the foe,
And, like true Norsemen, with nor fear, nor boast,
    Could die at post.

A deeper darkness falling on them fast,
    One brother fell at last ;
He found—his dead hand grasping still the oar,—
    Another shore.

Unclasping the dead fingers, their work done,
    The other struggled on ;
But quickly to the land of shadows dim
    He followed him.

The third took up their post, but all in vain,
And he, too, joined the twain,
And one was left to battle for the shore,
Brave Laurence Moar.

He reefs the little sail, and sets the mast,
A chance for life—the last ;
With one hand steers, the other bails the boat,
If she may float.

The water rises—can it be a leak ?
And he is growing weak.
The water rises—every nerve he strains—
It gains—it gains.

And still it gains, no more—no more a doubt,
The nile *—the nile is out.
Still undismayed ; he fought Death hand to hand,
And gained the land.

---

* A local term for the plug of the boat.

Did ever skipper bring such crew to shore

    As did brave Laurence Moar ?

Two dead—one saved—and now the roll of fame

    Has one more name.

DA SIMMER DIM.*

Da northern midnight simmer sky,
    Da waveless waters o' da voe,
Nae mortal een saw fairer scene—
    A heaven abune, a heaven below.
Nae soond is heard on land or sea,
    Owre a' sic saft light lingerin' lies
'At weel may seem a radiant dream
    Ta waft da soul ta Paradise.

An' fairer, dearer noo tae me—
    Ta me, dat noo maun laeve it a';
But I will brave da wildest wave,
    An' haud my hert, whate'er befa'.

---

* "Simmer dim"—the soft light of a Shetland night—if night it
can be called. Added to the charm of such a scene is the song of
the lark, heard half an hour after midnight.

My mither's last wirds fill her een,
    An' noo my father grips my haand—
" Gude's blessin' be attendin' dee,
    My boy, upon da sea or laand."

What hear I noo, high owre my head
'At comes, like hope, wi' wings ootspread ?
A voice, dat gars my twa een swim,
Da laverock, in da simmer dim.

.   .   .   .

Da stootest ship may come ta wrack,
    Da strongest back may hae ta boo,
Da bravest hert wi' life maun pairt,
    Sae I am lyin' lanely noo.
Last night in draem I wis at hame,
    A vision o' da happy past—
" Gude save my een ! Oh, hoo's du been ? "
    My mither cried—" Du's come at last."

" Come set de doun, du's cauld an' white,
    An' pit dy feet upo da paet ; "
" Naa mither, I maun geng da night,
    Da road is lang, da oor is late."

" Whaur—whaur da night, if it maun be?
    But du will sune come back, my ain ;"
" Naa, whaur I geng du'll come to me,
    An' den we'll never pairt again."

Dat midnight sky—dat waveless voe,
Da heaven abune, da heaven below,
An' noo—'sh—lack an angel hymn,
Da laverock, in da simmer dim.

RESTIN' DA FIRE.*

A SHETLAND FOLK SONG.

Da lang, lang day is wearin' troo ;
   Come gentle hümin † fa',
For faces, aye, an' voices noo,
   Are fadin' fast awa'.
Da hümin brings da night's dark wings,
   An' I'm begun ta tire ;
Da haand that kendled first my lowe
   Is restin' noo da fire.

Twa herts wer bright dat happy night,
   Da night 'at made us ane,
Twa herts an' haands we joined, an' noo
   We join twa haands again.

---

* Scottish equivalent—"Gathering the fire."
† Hümin—Twilight—Gloamin'.

Dat time we met, dis time we pairt ;
  But though I laeve dy side,
Du'll come ta me, den hert to hert !
  Oh ! winna we be blyde ?

I hear da far-aff skerries roar,
  'At fills da dark'ning sky,
Da dashin' wave apo da shore,
  Da sea-birds hamewird cry ;
An' I'm dat sea-bird seekin' hame,
  Gude grant me my desire ;
Sae sit by me, gudewife, an' see
  Da restin' o' da fire.

REVISITED.

A WAND'RER from the parent breast,
   Returning to the nest;
And Thule's rugged headlands rise
      To yearning eyes.

Grim outpost, where the wild winds sweep
   Along the midnight deep;
The hero of a thousand wars,
      And crowned with stars.

The stranger gives the tribute due,
   Dark sea caves, skies of blue,
And cliffs that tower to heaven above;
      I give thee love.

With sunlight breaks the silv'ry foam
   In music round my home,
And brings a song to my glad ears
      From far-off years.

Oh, brave old bard of tuneful lyre !
　　When wind and wave inspire,
What lay can match 'mid poet throng
　　　　Thy mighty song ?

The years are swept before the blast,
　　The present is the past,
And I am on thy heaving main,
　　　　A boy again.

With swelling heart I strain my sight
　　To where, in fadeless light,
All sea-enamoured, nestles down
　　　　My native town.

I seek the old house by the sea,
　　And enter rev'rently ;
It knows me not—all, all is change,
　　　　And I am strange.

Oh, could I find the little boy
　　Whose life had less alloy,
And look with his own eyes once more
　　　　On cliff and shore.

5

Revisited.

And eagerly each haunt I trace
That saw his beaming face;
Oh, cliff and shore! still unforgot,
I find him not.

VOICES.

OH, voices from the far-off seas,
   That break in song upon the shore ;
Oh, spirit of the summer breeze,
   With tender memories of yore.

Your gentle spell is over me,
   A dream of yearning heart and brain,
Across the mystic wave I see
   The days that were—return again.

'Neath Northern skies grim headlands rise
   'Mid roar of wave and flash of foam,
To listening ears and glistening eyes
   The sacred sounds and sights of home.

Lone Thule thy dread secret keep,
   Enough is told in rugged scars,
Bold warder of the midnight deep,
   Begirt with might and crowned with stars.

Another vision rises now,
   The school and playground on the hill,
And, 'mid the noise of restless boys,
   The master's voice—I hear it still.

We reared strong castles by the sea,
   And battles fought like Norsemen true ;
Is nothing left but memory ?
   Ah, brave companions !—where are you ?

The distant day in splendour lay,
   Where earth and sky in rapture met ;
But manhood smiled, for unbeguiled
   He saw the childhood glory set.

Sweet hope that comes, and slowly goes,
   What gain through all the rolling years ?
The flower of Wisdom buds and blows,
   When watered well with sorrow's tears.

Oh, voices from the far-off seas,
   That break in song upon the shore ;
Oh, spirit of the summer breeze,
   With tender memories of yore.

From sadder thoughts ye set me free,
   I feel the unforgotten near,
And loving arms enfolding me,
   And kisses Death makes doubly dear.

·

DA LAST NOOST.

("Noost" is the place to which a Shetland boat is drawn up in winter.)

A SANG, annider sang, ye say,
  An' if it be da last,
Need I be wae ? I'm haed my day,
  An' noo dat day is past.
My day is dune, what need I care ?
I'm haed him foul, I'm haed him fair ;
An sae, auld boat, for dee an' me
Nae mair, nae mair, da heavin' sea.

Du wis a boat o' boats da best,
  Troo mony a storm we drave ;
Noo in da Noost, du taks da rest
  We never mair will laeve.
Last haven, freend, for dee an' me,
For we're cross'd owre Life's changin' sea ;
We set oot wi' nae little trust,
An' noo it ends in dael an' dust.

When dee an' me, dat day in June,
   Broucht hame my bonnie bride,
My hert sung oot a blyde, blyde tune,
   Du danc'd ipo da tide.
Ah ! Life an' Love wis young, an' den
I haed a happy but an' ben ;
Du wis my pride ipo the sea,
An' she was da very hert o' me.

Den cam a day o' dule an' care,
   Da lift abune wis lead—
Across da dreary sea we bare
   To her last hame my dead.
My fecht is owre wi' wind an' wave,
Da Noost is noo da quiet grave ;
An' sae, auld boat, for dee an' me,
Nae mair, nae mair, da heavin' sea !

HUMANITY.

Music and beauty are now in the land,
  Glowing with gladness that knows no alloy !
Nature bestows with a bountiful hand,
  Revelling now in a rapture of joy.
Oh, could her joy, like a great river, flow
Down where the footsteps of misery go !

Fair is her face by the river and mead,
  Sweet is her voice on the land and the sea ;
Come to thy children, the sorest in need,
  Pining and dying, oh, mother, for thee ;
Enter love-laden the dwellings of woe,
Short is the season of respite they know.

Glory of dawn with the hope of the day,
  Glory of day in meridian of might,
Twilight the gentle, in garments of grey,
  Voice of eternity, marvellous Night ;

Wake the rapt soul to the longings and needs
Where the great heart of Humanity bleeds.

Mother of all, take the love that is thine,
   Thine shall it be till mine eyes shall be set,
Leaving to thrill all this being of mine,
   Love that is tenderer, mightier yet.
Sacred to hold, for Humanity's sake,
All through the night for the day that shall break.

SLEEP, MY LITTLE DARLING, SLEEP.

SLEEP, my little darling, sleep,
   Mother's arms no more shall hold thee ;
Wilt thou miss her loving kiss,
   Now the silences enfold thee ?
Summer sun and winter snow
Sweet one, thou wilt never know,
Free from all our anguish deep,
Sleep, my little darling, sleep.

Sleep, my little darling, sleep,
   Dark and dreary days we number,
Till that we with thee shall be,
   Wrapt in ever restful slumber ;
Joy and sorrow is our lot,
Time and change thou knowest not,
While we wake, and wake to weep,
Sleep, my little darling, sleep.

LOST LOVE.

Farewell, lost love, I will not say
  That falsehood dwells with thee,
But that the grave for evermore
  Hath hid my love from me.
And rendered back her spirit pure,
  As in the days of yore,
A star to light the darkest night
  Till night shall be no more—
     Oh, lost love,
     Oh, dead love,
  Till night shall be no more.

I will not tell my faithful heart
  Thy love was bought with gold ;
I only know the day is done,
  The night is dark and cold ;
So I will dream the tempter came,
  But death had been before ;

His kindly dart kept pure thy heart,
　　Mine own for evermore !—
　　　　Oh, lost love,
　　　　Oh, dead love,
　　Mine own for evermore !

I leave thee now, thy witching smile
　　May fall on whom it may,
For I will see thee nevermore,
　　But dream my dream alway.
I look on thee, and think of one
　　I loved in days of yore—
The form and face is all I trace,—
　　Farewell for evermore !—
　　　　Oh, lost love,
　　　　Oh, dead love,
　　Farewell for evermore !

THE GOOD AND THE TRUE.

THE night hath departed,
　The morning is here ;
Then welcome glad-hearted,
　The dawn of the year.

No sorrowful traces,
　Of days that are gone,
Shall darken our faces
　And shadow the dawn.

But fresh youth renewing,
　To dare, and to do,
And hopeful pursuing
　The good, and the true.

Oh greater the dower
　Than gold, or than lands,
Strong nerves flashing power
　To brain, and to hands.

With such a possession
  Inspiring the breast,
To cast down oppression,
  And raise the oppress't.

Unswerving and stoutly
  This pathway pursue,
And follow devoutly
  The good and the true.

IN MEMORIAM.

J. C.

A TRIBUTE to thy mem'ry, little friend,
  From one who feels a sympathetic sorrow
With those who mourn, and fail to comprehend,
  Yet seek from out the darkness, light to borrow.

We stand upon the cold and dreary shore
  Of that unfathomed, gloom-enshrouded ocean ;
We only hear the sobbing evermore,
  That sinks and rises with the waves' commotion.

Yet all the sunshine will not pass away
  That lighted thy sweet face, and filled thy spirit ;
Nor yet the sound of pattering feet at play,
  While we the boon of memory inherit.

The trembling stars of eve, the fairest flowers,
  The little warbling birds, the sunset's glory,
And every bright thing in this world of ours,
  Will keep forever now thy little story.

SONG OF THE SEASONS.

Set to music by Dr. JOHN GREIG.

Oh come bud-breathing Spring,
  With smiles that break through tears,
And bring, my loved one, bring
  The love that casts out fears ;
With budding beauties brighter than the day,
Oh love ! my love ! abide with me alway.

In leaf and flower arrayed,
  And song to give thee cheer,
Oh Summer, bright-eyed maid,
  The blossom of the year ;
The raptured breeze can neither go, nor stay !
Oh love ! my love ! abide with me alway.

The song has died away,
  And Summer now has gone,

Come Autumn, brown and grey,
    Dear heart, we two are one ;
With sober thought my hand in thine I lay,
Oh love ! my love ! abide with me alway.

Now bird and stream are dumb,
    And all the land is white,
Oh lonely Winter come,
    And bring the long, long night,
With peace and rest, for which the weary pray,—
Oh love ! my love ! abide with me alway.

HER PORTRAIT.

THIS truly is thy counterpart,
   I think it fair because like thee :
But what avails when my poor heart
   Will never, never more be free ?

And, like the slave that hugs his chains,
   I gaze, and fondly gaze again,
On that dear face where beauty reigns,
   And my escape is doubly vain.

Ah, me ! and whither shall he flee,
   Beholding once what I have seen ?
But evermore must think of thee,
   And what is now, and might have been.

The years have graven either brow—
   The brook where we stood side by side,
And kissed, and joined brave hands—is now
   A river, like an ocean wide.

THE ANNIVERSARY.

I HEAR his patt'ring feet upon the floor,
   And, shouting " Dada ! dada !" in his glee;
With wide-spread arms he meets me at the door,
   And now, with clasp and kiss, sits on my knee.

He tells me o'er his little griefs and joys,
   With such a pathos and a winning grace;
Entranced I hear the music of his voice,
   And see his whole soul beaming in his face.

And now he brings his picture-book again,
   And, pointing with his finger, tells anew,
With wonder working in his little brain,
   The myst'ries of each picture brought to view.

With sober questions, and with strange replies,
   He lays his dimpled little hand in mine;
And as I look within his radiant eyes,
   That strangely, with a far-off splendour, shine.

I tremble with a sense of coming ill,
    As if my little boy stood far apart.
"Oh, clasp me closely, darling !—closer still—
    The night hath brought a chill about my heart.

The shadows gather in my little room ;
    I rise from out the past, for you must know
That when the buds were bursting into bloom,
    My little darling died a year ago.

SUMMER.

A SONG—oh, a song to my love !
  The breezes are whispering her name ;
The sea, and the bright sky above,
  So changeful, yet ever the same,
    Her praises proclaim.

Her voice cometh over the sea,
  And breaks with the wave on the shore ;
The young hearts are shouting in glee,
  The old hear an echo of yore—
    An echo of yore.

And when at the dawn she is seen,
  Away from the town's busy throng,
In dew-spangled garments of green,
  All Nature breaks forth into song—
    Breaks forth into song.

And over green valley and hill
  Buds burst into bloom at her voice;
Before her the tempest is still,
  The grief-stricken hearted rejoice
      At sound of her voice.

A song—oh, a song to my love!
  Tears fall, but they fall not in vain;
The life-giving sunlight above
  Will strengthen and ripen the grain,
      Because of the rain.

IN THE SUNSHINE.

In the sunshine, little maiden,
　　Gather flowers while ye may,
Ere the Winter, tear be-laden,
　　Bid the blossoms all decay,
　　And the sunshine pass away.

Listen to the music ringing—
　　Bird and stream, and flowing sea,
With a thousand voices singing
　　All that wondrous melody
　　Sung through past eternity.

So that when the song is ending,
　　All thy inner senses may
Feel the music richly blending,
　　Calling back the Summer day,
　　And the sunshine pass'd away.

When at last the sun is setting,
　And the light is wearing grey,
There will be no vain regretting
　Of the short, short Summer day,
　And the sunshine pass'd away.

CRAZY JEAN.

"Oh, women, hae ye seen my bairn?
　I've sought him up an' doun;
Oh, women, hae ye seen my bairn?
　I've been through a' the toun.

I clad him in his tartan dress,
　An' pinafore sae white,
An' kissed him in my happiness,
　An' oh my heart was light.

An' oh my heart was light and free,
　My bairnie a' my ain;
Oh, think ye will I never see
　His bonnie face again?

He put his arms around my neck,
　An' pressed his lips to mine;

An' then I thought my heart would break
  Should I my bairnie tine.

They dress'd my bairnie a' in white,
  When day began to daw ;
An' when the day was shinin' bright,
  They took my lamb awa'.

They took my bairn, an' left wi' me
  A curl o' his bright hair ;
Oh, women, think ye, will I see
  His sweet face never mair ?

The frost is hard as ony airn,
  The wind is bitter cauld ;
Oh, wae's me on my bonnie bairn,
  My lamb within nae fauld !

I've sought him frae the break o' day,
  An' noo the day is dune,
An' shadows grey lie ilka way,
  An' angry clouds abune.

An' dark, dark night is gath'rin' fast,
    But that I winna mind,
For I will get sweet rest at last,
    When I my bairnie find."

   .   .   .   .   .   .

They found her, when the storm was past,
    Upon the frozen ground ;
And she has got sweet rest at last,
    And her lost bairnie found.

BROOMIEKNOWE.

THE hurry an' drivin',
The worry an' strivin',
The thousands wha under their daily cares bow,
The great city's clamour,
Its grandeur an' glamour,
I leave for the quiet o' sweet Broomieknowe.

There Nature adornin'
Hersel' wi' the mornin',
A bright dewy diadem circling her brow,
Awakens the flowers
Asleep in the bowers,
Whaur nestle the birdies at sweet Broomieknowe.

The birdies are singin',
The echoes are ringin',
An' deep are the echoes the heart has, I trow.

Yer een wi' tears glistenin',
Sae rev'rently listenin',
Ye'll hear its deep music at sweet Broomieknowe.

Oh, then the glad feelin'
Through ilka nerve stealin',
Yer spirit in rapt adoration will bow;
An' thrilled wi' the glory
Around ye an' o'er ye,
A new life will fill ye at sweet Broomieknowe.

The bright sky above ye,
A few friends that love ye,
A wee cosy cot on the side o' a howe;
There, after life's roamin',
Tae rest in the gloamin',
Sae calm an' sae peacefu' at sweet Broomieknowe.

ECHOES.

Oh, little flower, low bending thy young stalk,
  Oh, little birdie piping joyously,
Here as I meet you in my early walk,
  A flood of mem'ries rushes over me.

My own sweet flow'r-bud fresh with morning dew,
  My little birdie just begun to sing,
And while I gazed and felt a rapture new,
  The song was hushed, and nipt the blossoming.

Again the shadow creeps across my brow,
  The troubled waters rise and dim my e'e;
And as I see and hear you, even now,
  For his sweet sake, you both are dear to me.

THE TIME OF ROSES.

It was the time of roses,
We met, my love and I ;
And Beauty's hand had crown'd the land,
And music filled the sky.
Our souls were thrilled with rapture,
I know not how or why,
We wandered on by wood and stream,
And love was life, and life a dream,
Whate'er the spell
I know full well,
It was the time of roses
We met, my love, and I.

But when the first pale snowdrop
Was opening into flower,
My own ! my own ! was stricken down :
But saved from wind and shower
To keep my heart from breaking,
One little bud for dower.

One little bud—a tender care
From my dead flower that was so fair,
So I will trace
A vanished face,
When my own little snowdrop
Is opening into flower.

HOPE.

I SEE thee standing near, oh! bright-eyed one,
    I gather strength to run the life-long race ;
Around thy brow I see the light of dawn,
    And love triumphant in thy radiant face.

And thou wert with me in the early years,
    I followed thee through many pathways wild,
And worshipped thee, and had nor doubts nor fears,
    But all the strong faith of a simple child.

From early morn, till noon, and twilight grey,
    And when the,solemn stars looked down on night,
In midnight visions, waking dreams by day,
    I walked illumined by thy mystic light.

And in that early day the world was new,
    All wisdom dwelt, my father, then with thee ;
Oh simple faith ! oh simple faith and true !
    The shrine at which I knelt—a mother's knee.

7

Her gentle voice and eyes, angelic, mild,
　　Still follow me through all the rolling years ;
The bearded man looks back upon the child,
　　And though he smiles, his eyes are filled with teaı

He sees a land of sunshine and of flow'rs,
　　Receding far across an ocean wide ;
And all his soul is with the golden hours,
　　But now he hears Hope whispering at his side :

" Heed not the waning glory of the west,
　　But gird thyself to march and meet the dawn ;
And with a fearless heart within thy breast,
　　Through doubt and darkness, I will lead thee on.

THE COMIN' O' SLEEP.

OH, was there a bairnie like mine ever seen?
  It's past ten o'clock, an' my claes no in steep;
He looks in my face wi' his bright laughin' een,
  An' shouts oot a hearty defiance at sleep.

He ran oot an' in till the gloamin' cam' doun,
  His face and his hands wad hae fyled ony sweep,
I cleaned him, an' trampit the floor roun' an' roun',
  But a' to nae purpose, he'll no' fa' asleep.

I've tauld him I'm certain a score o' times owre,
  "The piggies that gaed to the market"—in vain,
His een that I lippen to close—only glower,
  An' aye he cries—"Mama! the 'piggies' again."

I warm his wee taes, but the bairnie's in grief,
  An' sobbin' you'd think his wee heartie would break;
He knuckles his half-closin' een wi' his nieve,
  An' stares in my face aince again, wide awake.

His een noo they close, noo they open again,
  But that, my wee man, was their last drowsy peep,
Though sairly ye fought, it has a' been in vain,
  Sae rest ye, my bairnie, fu' sweetly in sleep.

A cart, an' a pownie that wanted the head,
  He couldna abide to be oot o' his sight;
Nae ferlie, he wouldna lie doun in his bed,
  But grat in my arms nearly half o' the night.

And yet, my wee mannie, what else are we a',
  At last in that mystical darkness sae deep,
When faces an' voices are fadin' awa',
  But bairnies that greet at the comin' o' sleep.

"HUGO." *

THE storm is past and yet no calm I find,
 The night is over yet no dawn is here;
Although my waiting eyes with tears are blind,
 No comfort and no sweet relief is near.

I left my little boy upon the road,—
 He could not follow, and I could not stay:
Ah me! I could not ease him of his load,—
 But kissed him ere he sank down by the way.

I took his little hand within my own—
 I clasp'd him to my bosom where he lay,
And then I had to leave him all alone,
 And travel darkly on my dreary way.

The flowers bloom, but bloom no more for me,
 The skylark sings, his song fills not my ear,

---

* His pet name.

Oh ! for the face I never more shall see,—

    And that sweet voice I never more shall hear.

In visions only can my spirit trace—

    In dreams it comes to soothe my troubl'd mind

The dear resemblance of a treasured face,

    The echo of a voice left far behind :—

The voice I hear is calling unto me,—

    Beseeching arms stretch toward me as of yore ;

And now I stand beside a dreary sea,—

    The dark waves sobbing on the troubled shore.

I sit me down in darkness, and I weep,

    And still I cannot choose but travel on ;

Oh ! for the waking from this nightmare sleep !

    Oh ! for the breaking of a brighter dawn !

A close communion evermore I'll keep

    With thy young spirit, as I journey on,

And then mayhap—when I too fall asleep,

    I'll wake again, and meet thee at the dawn.

THE VIOLET.

Music by JOHAN S. SVENDSEN.

A DARK sky, cold and cheerless,
  The forest leafless, drear,
Yet with her blue eye fearless,
  The violet is here.

Bright pioneer upspringing,
  Defiant, sweet and true,
To earth in gladness bringing
  A part of heaven's blue.

Thou comest like one singing,
  A song of joys to come,
Thy lone voice clearly ringing,
  When all the land is dumb.

But Song and Beauty meeting,
  Our hearts then captive led,

The brighter days are greeting
And thou art lying dead.

Shall we, 'mid summer splendour,
Thy bright blue eye forget,
And no dear tribute render
To thee, sweet violet?

SONGSTERS OF THE GROVE.

Music by F. GUMBERT.

Oh, gladsome songsters of the grove,
   Ye fill the air with joy again,
Your thousand voices blend in love,
   And fall like soothing summer rain;
Ye hold me in a sweet control,
But boundless rapture thrills my soul,
That will abide with me alway,
   Oh go to her I love,
And tell her all my heart would say.

Oh roses, roses, bud and blow,
   The wind will waft your spirit there,
And sing birds sing, on joyous wing,
   The love I bear, the love I bear;
But linger, linger not in bliss,
Bring back from her own lips a kiss,
That will abide with me alway,
   Then go to her I love,
And tell her all my heart would say.

HEAVEN.

Do I believe in heaven ?   Yes,
　It burst upon my sight ;
I saw the sacred loveliness,
　I basked within the light.

I heard a voice from day to day
　Make music of my name,
And over all a glory lay
　That told me whence it came.

No city paved with shining gold,
　And jewels all bedight ;
The heaven I trace—a woman's face
　Aglow with love's own light.

A woman's heart, a woman's hand,
　For all life's ills atone ;
Her loving kiss, the raptured bliss,
　The paradise I own.

BY THE WAY.

Look here.
" At what ? a crow upon the roadside—dead ? "
He moves—the blood is oozing from his head ;
  Death's near.

  " Just so ;
And you would stand with melancholy eyes,
And over dying raven moralise,
  Poor crow !

  No more
Wilt thou for wife or little children rise,
And feed them, honestly, or otherwise,
  No more.

  No more
For thee (thy head laid lowly on the grass),
The cosy nest, and family, alas !
  No more.

By the Way.

No more"
Life!—death! whatever you may say, my friend,
Here lies what sages fail to comprehend—
    "No more"—

    Hush, see,
He moves his head! his wings now prostrate lie,
And such a human look within his eye.
    Ah! me.

    The strife
In growing darkness, and with laboured breath,
The rising, sinking, groping, grasping death,
    For life.

    The breath
Has gone—no! see, another, and another gasp—
Oh, God! once—once a loved one thus in grasp
    Of death

    I saw,
And, standing where this fellow-mortal lies,
My stricken soul comes trembling to my eyes
    With awe.

SONG OF THE PEOPLE.

OURS the learning by disasters,
  Ours the grief that maketh wise,
We, the people are the masters,
  Tyrants fall when we arise ;
Nurtured by long years of wrong,
We are ready, we are strong.

Ho ! my brothers we are strong,
  Hearts of all that would be free,
Never yet a nobler song,
  Led the way to victory,
On our banner line on line,
Freedom, Truth, and Progress shine.

Freedom ! all alike may share,
  Truth ! the pole star overhead,
Progress ! higher heights to dare,
  Battle cry might rouse the dead.

Ours the fight, our fathers fought,
Shall their strength be spent for nought?

Can we hold their mem'ry dear,
   Yet their sacred cause forego?
Let who will be dumb with fear,
   Braver spirits answer—no!
Not for class, or great, or small,
But the common good of all.

Rise! my brothers for the right,
   Rise! their day is past recall,
Galling fetters in our might
   Break asunder once for all,
Ours the hands shall clear the way,
Robe, and crown, the better day.

THE DYING YEAR.

GATHER round
  Where he lies;
Sleep profound
  Seals his eyes.

Hearken now,
  Final breath,
Darken'd brow,
  This is death.

Good or ill,
  Done before,
Cold and still,
  Evermore.

Solemn hour,
  This, the last,
Awful power,
  Present, Past,

Hearts may thrill
   As of yore—
Cold and still,
   Evermore.

Royal throne,
   Cot and hall,
Death alone
   Ruleth all.

Claspèd hands,
   Prayers nor tears,
His commands
   Interferes.

.   .   .   .

Night hath fled,
   Morning light,
Lay our dead
   Out of sight.

Selfish thrall,
   Hate, and spite,
Bury all
   Out of sight.

Doubt nor fear,
    Hope is strong,
Sweet and clear,
    Hear her song.

Wrong shall fail,
    Truth the pure
Shall prevail
    And endure.

Silken chain,
    Shore to shore,
Peace will reign
    Evermore.

MOTHERLESS.

SING, little darlings, in the twilight dim
   The hymn—your mother's hymn—
As on that night you sang to her you know,
       A year ago.

Come, Maggie—little housewife—you begin,
   And Jessie will join in;
And Laurence and wee Alick make the ring—
       Sing, darlings, sing !

They sing, and in their faces turned to me
   Their mother's face I see,
And in the voices falling on my ear
       Her voice I hear.

They sing, and dream-like, tender mem'ries rise,
   And fill my yearning eyes ;
A thousand loving deeds done out of sight
       Flash into light.

The oft-times weary hands and aching brow,
　　The longed-for rest, and now
The better day she toiled for come at last ;
　　　　　But she has pass'd.

The song is ended, and the day is dead,
　　And plllowed lies each head ;
To other hands are left the sleepers there,
　　　　　Her dearest care.

Oh, my own little darlings, do you miss
　　Your mother's nightly kiss ?
I know full well that but for your dear sake
　　　　　My heart would break.

When in the mazes of my troubled dream,
　　And Sorrow reigns supreme,
Come with the healing that your voices bring—
　　　　　Sing, darlings, sing !

THE LAST FIGHT.

HE left his home with failing hope and breath,
    To fight it out with Death ;
Death whispered, as he looked within his eyes,
    " A noble prize."

Where'er he went no land could give him life
    For such unequal strife :
At last, his one hope left—Death pressing nigh—
    Home ! home to die !

From morn till noon and night, from night till da
    The good ship hastened on ;
And hastened on the shadow o'er the tide,
    Nor left his side.

The happy earth-light faded in his eyes,
    And died, as daylight dies :
The silent valley opened unto him
    Its entrance dim.

Adown the valley, grasping now Death's hand,
    He heard the cry of—" Land ! "
And backward, upward to the light of day,
    He dragged his way.

And they that loved him met him on the shore,
    And kissed him o'er and o'er ;
He whispered, smiling, as his spirit pass'd,
    " Home ! home at last ! "

MAY.

Song in the bright sky above,
  Song on the glad earth below,
Breezes in rapture of love
  Tempting the roses to blow;
Voices come over the sea,
  Sweet as the voices of yore,
Come oh my love unto me,
  Dwell in my heart evermore.
Blossom anew 'neath the bountiful blue,
  Dwell in my heart evermore.

Robed with the beauty of day,
  Crowned with the glory of night,
Flowers that wait by the way,
  Break into bloom at thy sight;
Gone the wild wind and the rain,
  Gone the mad moan of the shore;

Come with thy bright eyes again,
Dwell in my heart evermore.
Blossom anew 'neath the bountiful blue,
Dwell in my heart evermore.

JUNE.

A BRIGHTER blue rejoicing sea and sky,
   A deeper green within the woods recesses;
With breath of morning and with beaming eye,
   Oh, come, sweet June, shake out thy golden tresses,
And drink the joy life-giving breezes bring,
Where roses blow, and woods harmonious ring.

We stray by flow'ry meads and babbling streams,
   And gladsome noon in garments white is shining,
The restless city knows thee but in dreams;
   Oh, could her children, in dark alleys pining,
But drink the joy life-giving breezes bring,
Where roses blow, and woods harmonious ring.

One star is rising in the cloudless blue,
   The silent herald of the sober gloaming,
To folding wings, and flowers bathed in dew,
   For day is done, and all too soon our roaming;
But we will sleep the darkening night away,
And dream again the rapture of the day.

LETHE.

HER hands were tightly clasped upon her breast,
   Her face was calm, like unto one in sleep,
And thus she lay (ah, who can tell the rest ?)
   Upon the bosom of the mighty deep.

Oh, fair young face, the rose too soon has fled ;
   Oh, gentle lips, the wanton waters kiss,
Oh, golden hair, a halo round thy head,
   And all that made thee dear, some home will miss.

The days will change to weeks, and months, and years,
   Yet, round the fireside hope will still remain,
And eyes will look the thought, through brightening
     tears,
   " Some day the wanderer will return again ! "

The stars looked down and trembled at the sight,
   The winds and waves their solemn burthen bore ;

The dawn beheld the wanderer still and white,
    And whispered, "Nevermore, oh, nevermore."

A queenly grace is seated on thy brow,
    Albeit now thine eyes have lost their glow ;
But tender love is even speaking now,
    On chin, and lips, and throat, like mountain snow.

Has love then led thee where the roses bloom,
    With music and with sunshine all thine own,
And left thee standing in a night of gloom,
    Amid dead leaves, and thy despair, alone?

Out, out upon the waters, cold and stark,
    Oh, wounded heart, is this thy healing balm ?
Alike to thee the sunlight and the dark,
    And heat and cold, the tempest and the calm.

Or hast thou seen the sudden tempest rise,
    And fearless men grow pale, and none to save,
And lifted up thy unavailing cries
    'Mid crashing wreck and all devouring wave ?

Our questions are but echoed back again—
    The lips are sealed, and sealed the speaking eye ;
We look, as mariners will look, in vain
    For light and guidance from a starless sky.

So farewell, vision, gloom and glory blent,
    Now fading from our wonder-stricken eyes ;
Live thou in memory a pictured saint
    Upborne on waves of bliss to Paradise.

NELLIE.

WHAT ails thee, little rosebud of my heart?
  The birds are singing in the sunny sky,
And yet my little one from all apart,
  Can only answer with a wailing cry.

The am'rous breeze but woos the gentle flow'rs
  To steal their souls, and wander heedless by;
We wait beside thee through the silent hours,
  Yet see we nought but sorrow in thine eye.

And like forget-me-nots bedrenched with dew,
  Thine eyes look strangely up from beds of snow;
Thine eyes look up—thy spirit shineth through,
  "Forget-me-not?" No, little darling, no!

The summer sunshine bids the heart rejoice,
  And earth, and sea, and sky in rapture meet;
When shall we hear the music of thy voice
  Keep happy time to little patt'ring feet.

Thy brother pauses in his lonely play,
 And with a wearied sigh, yet patiently,
" To-morrow," little darling, he will say,
 " Will Nellie rise ? and will she play with me ? "

" To-morrow," with its sunshine, never came—
 My little boy is standing by my side,
And clasping still the mem'ry of a name,
 With wond'ring eyes he whispers—"Nellie died."

Oh, sweet forget-me-nots, bedrenched with dew !
 Dear eyes that follow me where'er I go ;
Entreating still from death-calm depths of blue
 " Forget-me-not "—no, little darling, no !

SIC EST VITA.

From darkness unto darkness,
  Midway Life's ruddy glow,
A joy, a fear, a sigh, a tear,
  The sum of all we know.

From darkness unto darkness,
  With yet one brighter gleam,
The light that lies in Love's own eyes,
  A rapture, and a dream.

From darkness unto darkness,
  The wide, wide ocean o'er,
Yet not one sail will ever fail
  To find that silent shore.

A SALUTATION.

It wasna an Empress or Queen,
   That ken's o' a lang pedigree,
But a bairnie wi' bonnie blue een,
    That noddit to me.

Her ancestors landed, some say,
   In the Conqueror's guid company ;
She's conqueror noo, onyway,
    That noddit to me.

She rules, frae her gran'mither doun ;
   A darin' young despot is she ;
An' yet they wad gie her the mune,
    That noddit to me.

Nine months to a day was her age,
   Her height was at least twa fit three ;
An' just as a first coortin' stage,
    She noddit to me.

I then gat a kiss—let that pass,
  For she let them pass unco free ;
A fearless wee flirt is the lass
  That noddit tae me.

Then wba wadna say—when wi' pride,
  She wales wha her ripe lips will pree,
The bairnie will be a braw bride
  That noddit to me?

Be hers what a guid life will need,
  Till Death gently closes her e'e ;
An' lays doun the ance gowden heid
  That noddit to me.

Through mosses an' flow'r-sprangled dells,
  The Wanlock rows down to the sea ;
An' there amang fond hearts she dwells,
  That noddit to me.

GIORDANO BRUNO,

BURNT FOR ASSERTING A PLURALITY OF WORLDS, BY ORDER OF THE CHURCH, FEB. 1600.

" WITH greater fear you now pronounce my doom
  Than I unyielding take it from your hands."
He stood before them in the council-room
  Erect and free, despite their iron bands.

No cause he pleads upheld by people's voice,
  No fiery impulse heats a martyr's brain,
Alone and calm abides he by the choice
  Of weary years of bondage and of pain.

A page divine lay open to his sight ;
  He found the truth because he questioned why ;
And it was writ in characters of light
  A mighty marvel, on the midnight sky.

He followed truth ; proclaimed his purpose high
  With constant lips, and with unfalt'ring breath—

9

And in his deep devotion dared to die,   .·
 And Thought immortal triumphed over Death.

Some had supernal joys before their sight,
 And felt a Saviour's hand within their own ;
He had not this, but fought the final fight,
 And went into the darkness all alone.

Raise high the faggots ! ye would " shed no blood : " *
 Oh holy charity ! Oh Christlike grace !
Thought ye as 'mid the raging flame he stood,
 This damning lie would shield ye from disgrace !

He came, a greater gift than priest or king,
 Ye robed and crown'd him with devouring flame ;
Behold the rolling years avenging bring
 To you and to your heirs undying shame.

What need of monumental stone to thee ?
 Within the heart of truth art thou enshrined,
And in the heart of all that seek to free
 From priestly craft and creed, the bondaged mind.

---

* " Be merciful and shed no blood " is the horrible formula used in giving sentence of burning at the stake.

THE MYSTIC UNION.

I KNOW thy pale, pale face, and thoughtful brow,
  I've communed with thee in the silent hours,
And wept with thee, oh lonely one, and now
  I weave for thy sad brow a wreath of flowers.

A little child will twine it round thy head—
  A little bright-haired boy, with large blue eyes,
Where dawning genius such a light hath shed,
  As that up-springing through bright morning skies.

Enthroned art thou a queen, as sad as fair,
  And in my heart thou keepest royal state ;
So nothing base can ever enter there,
  Nor aught ignoble with thy nature mate.

Oh, in the paths of wisdom lead thou me,
  And I will follow, though my sight be dim ;
The homage, oh sweet sorrow, paid to thee,
  Is part of that deep love I bear to him.

For now a mystic union joins us twain
  That will abide, like everlasting truth ;
And so in mem'ry free from any pain
  He lives for ever in eternal youth.

He climbs upon my knee, I hear him speak,
  I feel his clasping arms about my neck ;
And then I smile, and tears are on my cheek,
  And but for this, I think, my heart would break.

HER BIRTHDAY.

My little lady entering on her teens,
　Has sent me warning of her birthday time.
And if I guess not what the maiden means,
　I still will find a shelter for my rhyme.

In darkest hour, like peace it comes to me,
　And so I cherish it as heaven-sent,
And if my verse gives hope and strength to thee,
　My little lady, I shall be content.

The thoughts, too high for any human words,
　In music only do their numbers roll,
Vibrating deep, and universal chords,
　The internationality of soul.

So in the spring and budding of thy youth,
　Whatever new necessities arise,
Yea, even with the homage paid to truth,
　Thy gift of music reverently prize.

Let not the idle censure of the throng,
  Nor too fond praises of the favoured few,
Break in upon the cadence of thy song,
  But steadfastly to thy own soul be true.

A deeper joy from contemplation caught,
  Exceeding far what praise of men impart,
When all thy skill is spent to shape the thought,
  The finer essence still eluding art.

The flower will bloom, remote from human sight,
  The lark will soaring sing, though none are near,
The stars in heaven shine in cloudy night ;
  So sing all careless thou how few may hear.

Light—inward light—will fill thy longing eyes,
  And thrill thy being with a sweet control,
As thought on thought for utterance arise,
  To melt in music through thy raptured soul.

FELO DE SE.

ENGLAND IN THE NINETEENTH CENTURY.

A Fact.

WHAT do I know of deceased lying here?
  Feeble he was, sir, but willing to work;
Fourpence a-day—it may sound kind o' queer,—
  That was his wage, sir, from daylight till dark.

Workhouse? well, no, sir; he oft would complain
  Master and matron had used him so ill;
Never, he said, would he go in again,—
  Never, leastways, would he go with his will.

Yet, sir, he slept in an outhouse o' nights,
  Hard on an old man, and feebler he grew;
Aye! and his eyes used to kindle wi' lights
  Strange in the face of the man that we knew.

Felo De Se.

Last time I saw him—the last time in life—
    Gave him a supper, he needed it so,
Children came round him,—he spoke of his wife,
    Seemed to forget she was dead long ago.

Where did I find him?—why, hung to a beam,
    There in the outhouse, a kind o' a shed ;
Scarce could I think it was aught but a dream,
    Quickly I took him down, and—he was dead.

        Gentlemen, now,
          Do ye agree?
        Verdict allow—
          Felo de se.

Now, uncoffined, fling him on the cart,
        This the law demands,
Night, dark night, must fitting aid impart
        To your hands.
Bring the rope, and tie to neck and feet,
        Drag the grey-haired man,
Fling him in, and to your brother mete
        Church's ban.

Yet a little farther ye can go,
      Lay him south and north,
East and west, for you, that men may know
      Christian worth.
Foolish people, this man never knew
      Of your Church's deeds ;
Death, his friend, comes in and laughs at you,
      And your creeds.

GARIBALDI.

" AND is the victor vanquished at the last?
　　And has his spirit passed?"
" Triumphant still," is Death's reply—
　　" He cannot die!

" He cannot die while Freedom shall but own
　　One human heart for throne—
　A terror still to tyranny
　　His name shall be.

" Wherever suffering people make a stand
　　For love of fatherland,
　There shall his dauntless spirit lead
　　In sorest need.

" There shall dread war be even glorified,
　　Wherever he shall guide,
　Because his sword is drawn for thee,
　　Oh Liberty!

" So gather round me all the good and true,
  Who faint not, but pursue
 The upward march from height to height,
   To purer light.

" The sounding titles born of pomp and state,
  And heralded as great,
 Are swept away as empty chaff
   With honest laugh.

" What title, then, for guerdon shall I give,
  That shall forever live ? "
" There is no higher honour than
  The title Man ! "

" With his name," Freedom cries, " shall mine be wed,
  Till Freedom shall be dead !
 Henceforward, through all time, we twain
   As one shall reign ! "

SHALL WE BIND THE CHAIN.

" HELP ! oh help ! shall Freedom die ? "
" No ! " the Cossack makes reply.
" What though all men else be dumb,
" Brother, ho ! we come ! we come ! "

Over mountain, ice, and snow,
Deeply sworn to strike the blow ;
Death ! or Freedom ! on they go,

On resistless as thy tide,
Mighty Danube ; far and wide,
Sweep they down the Tyrant's pride.

Shall we stem that tide,
Freedom's rushing river ?
Wake again the strife ?
Give oppression life ?
Never ! never ! never.

Battle-drum is heard no more,
Clash of swords, nor cannon's roar ;
But the wail above the dead
Pierces through the gloom o'erhead.

" Has the storm and darkness gone ?
When—oh when, will break the dawn ? "
Cry they, still with tearful moan.

Hearing that beseeching cry,
Shall the hope within them die ?
Brothers—what shall we reply !

  Shall we bind the chain
   Blood and tears now sever ?
  Wake again the strife ?
  Give oppression life ?
   Never ! never ! never !

MICHAEL SERVETUS.*

" OH wretched man ! will not my goods and gold

    Buy wood enough to end my misery ?

Still, still I live, and yet the hours have rolled

    A century of torment over me."

So died for Truth, Servetus, hunted down

    By Protestant Reformers Calvin-led ;

---

* Calvin and Servetus had maintained an amicable correspond-
ence for 16 years, when on certain doctrinal points Servetus argued
so successfully as to engender Calvin's jealous hatred.   On the
strength of these private letters, and other papers obtained by
Calvin in no honourable way, Servetus was arrested, but escaped
from prison, and resolved to retire to Naples.   He took his route
through Geneva.   Calvin set the authorities upon him, and he was
again arrested on a charge of heresy and blasphemy, the main
charge being : " That in the person of Mr. Calvin, minister of the
word of God in the Church of Geneva, he had defamed the doctrine
that is preached, uttering all imaginable injurious and blasphemous
words against it."   Calvin was the accuser, and according to law
he would have been required to surrender himself to abide the
penalty should the charge be proved false.   Calvin sent his
domestic in his place.   Servetus after enduring a painful imprison-
ment was condemned to be burnt alive on the 27th October, 1553.
Historians are agreed that the dreadful sentence was pronounced
at the instigation of Calvin.

Oh fools ! ye gave to him a fiery crown *
    A crown of glory that will never fade !

John Calvin, trusted friend ! oh can it be
    That everything but hate is now forgot ?
Then wallow in thy depth of infamy,
    More foul and loathsome than Iscariot.

Thy cruel creed is swept into the night—
    The brutal outcome of a brutal mind ;
But what is lost in quenching this one light,
    Through all the rolling years we may not find.

Because this man is great, as thou art small,
    His name is far above thy poisonous breath ;
Thy spirit cannot keep his soul in thrall,
    Servetus lives ! and thou hast died the death !

Triumphant satire, laugh with lip of scorn !
    Geneva ! home of Reformation ! thou !
For Truth's sake slayest Truth ; now sit forlorn,
    Betrayer ! Coward ! blazoned on thy brow.

---

* Sulphur was actually put round his head to add horror to the scene.

I DO NOT KNOW.*

WHEN early faith, drawn from a mother's lips,
By calm-eyed Reason suffers an eclipse—
  Uphill thy path and slow.
When friends importune thee, "where dost thou go?"
Enough for thee if Reason lead the way.
Right onward; teach thy tongue to say,
  "I do not Know."

Read thou the Scripture, say they, light thou'lt see;
But if their light be darkness unto thee,
  By word and act then show,
That true, as to the ocean-rivers flow,
So true art thou to Reason's royal sway.
What is beyond her, teach thy tongue to say
  "I do not Know."

---

* Teach thy tongue to say, "I do not Know." *A Hebrew precept.*

And one by one thy friends may know thee not,
Or think of thee as one to be forgot;

      Then stronger thou shalt grow,

As lonely trees do when the tempests blow,
So thou art true, this friend is friend for aye :
Aught lovelier?   Oh, teach thy tongue to say,

      " I do not Know."

A time will come, a time to thee of rest,
And in thy weariness it will be best ;

      If voices whisper low,

Is aught beyond this sad sunsetting glow?
While night falls gleamless of another day,
Fear not the darkness, teach thy tongue to say,

      " I do not Know."

RE-CONSECRATED.

(A Fact.)

HE crept within the house of God
  And hid among the carving,
The strange old man had no abode,
  And he withal was starving.

For he had seen his fellow men
  Pass by, his wants unheeding ;
Without was din, but here within,
  The quiet he was needing.

So day by day concealed he lay,
  Companioned by his sadness ;
Or whether there, it was despair,
  Or whether it was madness.

But while to call good folks to prayer
  The bell was loudly clanging,

The beadle passed, and stood aghast,
   To find a man was hanging.

They cut him down, and through the town
   The thing was long debated,
But all agreed to have with speed
   The church re-consecrated.

STEADFAST AND STRONG.

ENTHRONED above all earthly din and strife,
    Enshrined within our hearts thy memory lies,
The record of a pure and noble life,
    That looked abroad with sympathetic eyes.
For life was more than worldly loss or gain,
The mystery, the pleasure, and the pain.

From early dawning of the morning light
    To where the noon and twilight shadows blend,
And ever onward to the falling night,
    Thou hast been brave, and faithful to the end;
The light of love within illumined thee,
Steadfast and strong for all humanity.

They who beheld thee from a distance knew
    Devoted duty crowned thy honoured years;
They give esteem and admiration due,
    But we—the loving tribute of our tears;
Life, love, and death, through all thy heart was str[
And thy whole being was a noble song.

THE BAIRNIE'S PIECE.*

"HERE, sir," she said, and laid it in my hand,
   And I, not knowing, asked her, "What is this?"
"The bairnie's christening piece," she answered, and
   I smiled and give the rosebud lips a kiss.

I thought I saw the shadow of a tear;
   Her heart was full, her mother's joy complete;
She said, "The baby's name is Willie Weir,"
   And so we parted on the silent street.

I caught contagion from the mother's eyes,
   Her tender voice and look had softened me;
What marvel, then, that I should moralise
   On this, her item of humanity?

---

* When children in Scotland are taken to the church to be baptised it is the custom for the mother to carry a piece of cheese and cake, which she offers to the first person met on the way.

A right good welcome to thee, Willie Weir,
　　To this strange earth of ours, and motley race,
And may thy mother shed no sadder tear
　　Through thee than that one beaming on her face.

This Scottish custom speaks the peoples' mind,
　　For surely with the people it began ;
A kinship claimed, embracing human kind,
　　And there we have the brotherhood of man.

PARTED.

THE song is sung, the tale is told,
    Farewell delusive dreaming;
The heart I thought so warm is cold,
    And love was only seeming.
Where lies the blame? I only know
    I waken from my dreaming.

And now farewell! 'tis better we
    Should part to-night for ever;
The friendship you desire of me
    Can live in our hearts never.
The blow-that broke the strongest tie
    All other ties must sever.

And so they parted years ago,
    She only then discerning
A stream that had a deeper flow,
    A heart a deeper yearning;
And he, his youthful hopes laid low,
    A nobler manhood earning.

WASHIN' DAY.

THE morning rase wi' sunshine bright an' fair,
　　But syne cam' doun a cauld an' drizzly weet;
An' Sandie Scott, like ane oppressed wi' care,
　　An' sair be-draigled, hammer'd up the street.

It wasna what ye ca' a right doun-pour,
　　But a'thing might hae been drawn thro' the sea:
The lift abune was mirky, glum, an' dour,
　　An' Sandie Scott, the very same was he.

His nieves were in his pouches, elbow-deep,
　　Ilk foot cam' like a cause'ay beater doun;
His bonnet sloped an' gar'd the water dreep,
　　A scarlet tassel dangl'd frae the croun.

"Gude mornin', Sandie," quo' lang Tam M'Dowal;
　　"What think ye, man, is it no gaun tae fair?"
"Gude mornin'!" answered Sandie, wi' a growl;
　　"I hope ye're satisfied, ye hae yer share."

"What ails ye, man? but ye're a saucy chiel',
   That ye wad answer onybody sae !
Ye look as if ye'd seen the very deil,
   An' had a collieshangie wi' him, tae."

"Ay, waur than that, I've fed on taties cauld,
   An' caulder kail, for twa lang mortal days ;
My hoose a ruin, like a century auld ;
   My wife, wi' face o' thunder, trampin' claes ;

The laddies, speelin' like wild beasts let loose,
   Owre hills an' mountains o' the dirty duds ;
An' every bite I tak' within the hoose,
   The very taste an' smell o' soapy suds."

" Hoots, man, awa', that's no worth sic a sang,
   Ye're naethin' waur than ither folks for that ;
I left my wifie an' her mither thrang
   A-liftin' in oor blankets drippin' wat."

"Well, Tam, I try tae dae the best I can,
   But this I ken, whatever folks may say,
He just maun be a maist courageous man
   Wha has the heart tae laugh on sic a day."

FAIR AN' FAUSE.

Tune--"She's Fair an' Fause."

Oh, fair an' fause, sweet love is dead,—
  The saddest death o' a',
A cauld, cauld heart is his death-bed,
  Sae let the dark night fa'.
Oh, brightest beauty man can bear !
Oh, rapture deein' in despair !
But I'll remember evermair
  The love-light noo awa'.

We part forever, thou and I,
  The saddest death o' a',
Without a tear, without a sigh,
  Sae let the dark night fa'.
Oh, sweetly fause ! oh, fausely fair !
My heart was dreamless o' a snare,
But I'll remember evermair
  The love-light noo awa'.

THE CAULD BLAST.

"OH, wert thou in the cauld blast,"
   She sang wi' me, she sang wi' me ;
Wi' breakin' heart I sang my pairt,
   " I'd shelter thee, I'd shelter thee,"
For even then, beyond, a' power
Was drivin' on the deadly shower :
An' oh ! the face that looked on me
Will never leave me till I dee.

Oh, sunless shower ! oh, bitter blast !
   Nae help could be, nae help could be,
An' so the pang lay in the sang—
   " I'd shelter thee, I'd shelter thee."
Cauld, cauld thy lips—my ain, my ain,
An' burnin' kisses fa' in vain ;
A lanely, lanely heart I'll bear
For evermair, for evermair.

NIGHT.

Oh hush thee darling, clasp me tight,
   There's hunger in thy cry;
For thee! for thee! my child, to-night,
   How gladly would I die!

Cold, cold and dark, nor moon, nor star
   To light me from above;
But colder still, and darker far,
   The heart of faithless love.

His honeyed words, his broken vow,
   His kisses on my lips,
Oh how my being loathes him now,
   Yea to the finger tips.

Despair, and hate, my comrades wild,
   Love only then I knew;
Thy cry will drive me mad, my child;
   Oh God! what shall I do?

I hear the moaning of the wind,
   The waves upon the beach ;
Oh can ye calm a troubled mind ?
   The depths of my woe reach ?

Oh dark, dark waters calm and deep,
   My soul ye have beguiled,
And I could on your bosom sleep
   But—Oh ! my child ! my child !

Who—who would tend thee little one ?
   What mother would'st thou find ?
I dare—and dare not, go alone—
   Say—am I cruel or kind ?

One kiss—one long, long kiss—the last ;
   We go into the night ;
The pain of it will soon be past,
   My darling ! clasp me tight.

MORNING.

OVER the sea and the land,
   Morning—the angel of light ;
And on the wet shining sand,
   Death—the pale offering of night.

Whiter is she than the foam,
   Colder is she than the sea ;
Here she hath sought her a home,
   Here with her babe she is free.

Free from the love that was sweet,
   Free from the life that was new,
Hither she came with sad feet ;
   Death—her last friend—she found true.

Clasping her little one tight,
   Nay, do not take them apart ;
So went they into the night,
   Cheek press'd to cheek, heart to heart.

'Mid so much music and light,
   Oh, was there not anywhere
One little hope that was bright ?
   One hope to save from despair ?

Silence and shadow of night,
   Here on the wet shining sand ;
Morning—the angel of light
   Over the sea and the land.

CAN I FORGET?

THE hope that filled our morning skies,
  The happy day that rose and set,
The light that faded from your eyes
  Can I forget? can I forget?

The one dear heart that followed you,
  Two little darlings round me yet,
Stir depths of love I never knew,
  Can I forget? can I forget?

Their father's face in theirs I see,
  They soothe and keep alive regret,
A thousand ways they speak to me,
  Can I forget? can I forget?

Oh, last sad hour, your spirit passed,
  Oh, first glad hour—the hour we met—
And oh, the first kiss, and the last!
  Can I forget? can I forget?

HIS LAST SONG.

A YOUTHFUL poet dying lay,
  His new-made bride attended near ;
Before the dawning of the day
  This song he whispered to her ear.

The singing time of birds has come,
  And flowers open gladsome eyes ;
My singing lips are almost dumb,
  And all that once was, slowly dies.

My heart is like a troubled sea
  That breaks against a rocky bar ;
You say sweet rest will come to me,
  Ah, yes ! but love is sweeter far.

I see you smile through gathering tears,
  To hide from me your heart of pain ;
Before me rise the bygone years,
  With joys that come not back again.

11

See ! see ! the glorious dawn is here,
  And see ! my fading morning star ;
Yea, rest is sweet, and rest is near,
  But love—ah, love ! is sweeter far.

BE NEAR, SWEET HOPE.

(MELODY BY HAYDN.)

OH, weary heart, night's shadows flee,
Bright morning breaks on land and sea,
Flowers ope their eyes, glad songs arise,
Where is thy voice—thy voice,
When bird and flower rejoice?

Thou bringest rest, oh, peaceful night,
We sleep but wake—wake with the light;
Will night, dark night, bring morning bright?
Dark, dark the way we grope,
Oh, be thou near, sweet hope.

Earth weeps her dead in Winter rain,
But radiant Spring brings life again;
Oh, Death, shall we find life through thee?
Dark, dark the way we grope,
Oh, be thou near, sweet hope.

Be Near, Sweet Hope.

Come! come! when day sinks into night,
When strength shall fail with failing light;
Eyes closing fast shall look their last,

And through the dark we grope,

Oh, then! be near, sweet hope.

MOTHER.

I DREAMT I knelt in tears beside your bed ;
   You whispered, as the darkness deeper grew,
" My arms—your neck—" and then your spirit fled,
   And I awoke, and found my dream was true.

But round my neck your weary arms I twined,
   And held you face to face a moment free,
Then one last kiss, while Love and Death combined
   To look with your own eyes and smile on me.

Oh, first glad eyes that met my dawning sight,
   Oh, first sweet voice that filled my wak'ning ears,
Your deathless music and your fadeless light,
   Will follow me through all the rolling years.

When higher thoughts within my being rise,
   And nobler actions follow in their train,
I feel the light of your inspiring eyes,
   I hear the music of your voice again.

THROUGH THE YEARS.

THE day is dune, the frost an' snaw is lyin' ilka gate ;
Draw in your chair, my ain gudeman, and you, de[
Aunty Kate ;
We'll wyle awa' an' hour or twa, nor think the hour w
tyne
In wanderin' owre the gate again we wandered ow[
langsyne.

The meadow green is no the same, nor yet the hawthor
glen,
Whaur we ha'e watched the stars come oot—but w
were sweethearts then ;
We quarrelled whyles, an' kissed again, mair fain f[
what had been ;
Noo three old folk sit smilin' here, though tears are i[
their een.

When Katie's Willie said farewell, the pairtin' was fu'
  sair,

He sailed awa', the ship was lost, she never saw him
  mair ;

Ah, little ken we, though the smile upon her face is seen,

The licht frae oot a sunset sky is fillin' baith her een.

Oor first, wee rompin' Willie, wi' his big bricht een o'
  blue,

Got his last kiss, an' lies fu' still aneath the daisies noo ;

An' sweet wee Nellie, like a star, gaed oot at mornin'
  daw ;

Oh, lang, lang dowie is the hoose whaur hame-licht is
  awa'.

Oh, sunlicht memories, dear to age, ye come in broken
  gleams,

As visionary noo, as cam oor youthfu' rosy dreams,

The day is dune, an' hand in hand we wait for nicht to
  fa' ;

The fire is failin' on the hearth, an' sune will dwine awa'.

ASLEEP.

My little boy is sleeping,
  While bright the morning breaks ;
His mother she is weeping,
  Her darling never wakes.

And 'tis so all beguiling,
  Wild hope our sorrow takes ;
He lies so sweetly smiling,
  We almost think he wakes.

Let sweet peace fill our dwelling,
  His sleep is of the best,
No tempest round him swelling
  Will ever break his rest.

Is't well to wish him other?
  We thank thee for his sleep,
O everlasting mother !
  Lest waking he might weep.

Come then, and kiss him sleeping,
  So still, so pure, and bright,
Why stand ye round him weeping,
  Kiss him and say good-night.

He lies from ills defended,
  He fears nor heat nor cold,
His merry song is ended,
  His little tale is told.

WAR.

An Incident of the Egyptian Campaign.

" The infidel invader we must fight—
    Allah, defend the right !—
And drive him from the land.   Then, then, my sweet,
    Shall we not meet ? "

" Ah, yes, I know ; but oh, my heart ! my heart !
    We cannot, cannot part.
My boy and I, whatever Fate decree,
    Will go with thee.

Disguised beside thee, who shall ever know
    A woman meets the foe ?
This boon I crave thee, that we share thy lot ;
    Deny me not."

The camp of Egypt slumbered on, nor knew
    The Fate that nearer drew ;

No note of warning sounded through the gloom,
　　Of coming doom.

The midnight march of Death, in silence deep,
　　The yell that roused from sleep,
The wakening to close the startled sight
　　In deeper night.

Within the foremost trench together lay,
　　Death-struck at dawn of day,
Two soldiers and a boy, and, breast to breast,
　　Had sunk to rest.

AUNTIE JEAN.

WHEN ye gang to see the Eildon hills, whaur I sae fai
    wad be,
Bring me back a sprig o' heather, naething mair I'll as
    o' ye ;
It will be a dear remembrance, it will fill my thirsı
    een—
Oh, ye little ken the treasure it will be to Auntie Jean.

For my heart will leave the city, wi' its endless hous
    and street,
An' I'll wander round sweet Gattonside wi' unencun
    bered feet ;
An' my faither an' my mither, an' oor cosy hame ǎ
    night ;
An' the Tweed an' a' its bonnie banks will rise i
    hallowed light.

Weel I mind when I a lassie, ere I entered on my teens,

Took the road frae oot the city, leaving a' my best o'
freen's ;

An' for mony a lang, lang mile I gaed wi' hamesick
heart fu' sair,

But I said—" Oh, bonnie Melrose, I will leave ye never
mair."

I was brought back in a kindly cairt, fu' weary an' fu'
wae,

An' though threescore years hae flitted by, it's fresh as
yesterday ;

An' the feelin' only deepens, that my een wad like to
see

Just a sprig o' heather frae the spot whaur I sae fain
wad be.

Wi' her last words in my ears I climbed my auntie's hill
wi' pride,

An' hooever strange it seems, I felt her presence by my
side ;

Sae we knelt doun on the hillside, for I kent we we
    together,
An' wi' reverent hand I plucked for her a sprig
    bloomin' heather.

To the city wi' a lightsome heart my treasure hame
    bore,
But I kent, whene'er they let me in, that Death had be
    before ;
To the darken'd room they led me, wi' a whispered
    " Come and see,"
An' the sprig o' heather in my hand brought tears
    every e'e.

We remembered, in the stillness that surrounds t
    perfect rest ;
Sae we laid the sprig o' heather in her hand upon h
    breast ;
An' her faither, an' her mither, an' the cosy hame
    night,
An' the Tweed, an' a' its bonnie banks, arose in h
    lowed light.

A BROTHER BARD.

WE met, and walked a little space, and now
   I see thee lying in thy lowly rest,
Pale silent lips, closed eyes, and darkened brow;
   And I am dumb, who knows it may be best?

The flowers are coming forth to welcome Spring,
   The singing time of birds is now at hand;
A tender memory to us they bring,
   For thou art gone into the silent land.

And we shall miss thy voice along the way,
   So much less music on our ears will fall:
The great world rushes on from day to day,
   One singing heart is silent, that is all.

The song is hushed that was so well begun,
   To add a name to unfulfilled renown;
And now we come with tears, when day is done,
   To leave on thy dead brow the poet's crown.

CHRIST IN BONDS.

" HE came, and yet His own received Him not,"
    We read in ancient lore,
For Truth and Freedom's sake He chose His lot,
    And suffering bore.

" The foxes have their holes, the birds of air
    Their nests, and yet," He said,
" The Son of Man He hath not even where
    To lay His head."

Oh, Truth ! oh, Freedom ! is it gain, or loss,
    Ye count the Christmas morns ?
For love of you, He bore the bloody cross,
    And crown of thorns.

Behold ! ten thousand temples reared on high
    To Christ of Nazareth,
And there, the heirs of Freedom, creed-bound lie
    In living death.

Oh, Satire ! greater never saw the light,

    A people still in chains

Who cry from out the darkness of their night :

    " Christ Jesus reigns ! "

LIGHT OF LOVE.

OUR morning rose with sunshine and with song,
   And all our being thrilled with love's own joy
We looked upon a world without a wrong,
   We felt a happiness without alloy;
Then came the very life of our own life,
   A tender blossom, pure as Alpine snows;
Companion of my pilgrimage—dear wife,
   What day-dreams in our happy home arose?

Our morning rose with sunshine and with song,
   But long ere noon our sky was overcast,
Yet we—we feared not, for our love was strong,
   Until we saw our flower fading fast.
She grew within the garden of our heart,
   No brighter blossom gladdened human sight,
She died, but in our soul—the dearest part—
   She lives for evermore, in love's own light.

LIFE.

A LITTLE pain, a little pleasure,
   From day to day new care and strife,
Of all, mayhap, an equal measure,
   So passes on our little life;
So little learned, so little won,
'Tis ended ere 'tis well begun.

At morning dawn how long the way,
   At noon we gather weeds and flowers,
At eventide we fain would stay,
   But swiftly onwards speed the hours;
And then, ah ! then, the setting sun
Proclaims our little day is done.

A CENTENARIAN.

Λ MOMENT pause along the way of life,
  A breathing space amid our hopes and fears ;
We think the way is long, and hard the strife,
  Our friend has battled on a hundred years.

And so to-night he sits our honoured guest,
  And so full-heart fraternal greetings flow,
For though the light is waning in the west,
  The morning rose—a hundred years ago.

The morning rose, and brought the world-old fight,
  That comes as surely as with life the breath ;
From babyhood, and on to manhood might :
  With all the weal and woe of love and death.

Oh, may the days fall gently—and all-good
  Abide with you until the end—and we
" The old time honoured " mystic brotherhood
  With hearts and glasses full—pledge three times t

A VALENTINE.

ALICE ; shall I say *my* Alice ?
May I drink from Love's own chalice ?
   Lips—dear lips of thine.
Eyes that flash out fitful sallies,
Love's Aurora Borealis,
While with my poor heart he dallies,
Down in mis'ry's deepest valleys
   Sinks this soul of mine.

Ah, how can you still be callous ?
What avails 'gainst Fate's fell malice
Heart as brave as Bruce or Wallace ?
Habitant of cot or palace
   In despair must pine,
Like the slave on Roman galleys ;
Then ! ah, then, angelic Alice,
   Be my valentine !

JENNIE DUNN.

A FORTNIGHT yestreen,
Frae twa bonnie een,
My puir heart has got sic' a stun,
I loathe meat an' drink,
An' sleep no' a wink
Wi' thinkin' o' sweet Jennie Dunn.

Her snawy white broo,
Her cheek an' her mou',
An' then her wee sweet dimpled chin,
Are a' sae combined,
Beseigin' my mind,
Nae rest can I find oot or in.

Her een are sae bright,
They dazzle the sight;
Her locks are like beams o' the sun;

Whaever he be,

Whose heart is yet free,

Has never yet seen Jennie Dunn.

Frae 'neath her lang lashes

Shoot heartbreakin' flashes,

They only escape them who run.

A closer acquaintance

Wad bring sure repentance

To him wha wad woo Jennie Dunn.

For every new lover

That tried yet to move her,

Just ended where he had begun ;

And nae fascination

Made ony impression—

Heart-free aye remained Jennie Dunn.

Wi' huntin' her here,

An' huntin' her there,

Ae chiel wore oot three pair o' shoon ;

An' nae mortal born

Was half sae outworn

As he when he left Jennie Dunn.

An' noo, I suspect,

Our ways to correct,

An angel has come frae abune

To torture the mind

O' wicked mankind,

An' christened hersel' Jennie Dunn.

PEACE OR WAR?

AND we had deemed the storm of war was past,
  And peace had come at last ;
And that the earth, above her thousands slain,
  Would bloom again :

That Freedom, struggling through the suff'ring years
  With agony of tears,
Would sit enthroned among the sons of men,
  And joyful reign.

But no—we hear the cry, " To arms ! to arms ! '
  " Give spread to war's alarms,
And let no more the voice divine be heard,
  But draw the sword ! "

A nation bruised and bleeding from the strife,
  Bereft of half her life,
In bravely waging warfare for the right,
  Are we to fight ?

Oh, Britain, save thyself while there is time
From folly worse than crime;
Scotland, at least, for sake of the opprest
Will still protest.

THE DYING YEAR.

Out of the infinite vast,
   Into the heart's loving light,
Friends ! oh, my friends of the past !
   Welcome ! oh, welcome to-night.

Join with the few that remain,
   Death shall not keep you in thrall ;
Love will not call you in vain,
   Love that is stronger than all.

Story and song shall go round,
   Tribute of smile and of tear ;
Hearts disunited be bound,
   Conquest to honour the year.

Hush ! he is nearing his end,
   Yet, ere he passes from sight,
Gather around our old friend,
   Give him a solemn—Good-night.

Hark! to the low monotone;
. Hark! to the labouring breath,
Coming and going with moan,
   Marking the footsteps of Death.

Never a light in the west,
   Never a star overhead;
Fold ye his hands on his breast,
   Close ye his eyes—he is dead.

Dead! and the hope, and the fear,
   Love, or the hate that we bore,
Now hath gone out with the year,
   Sealed in his heart evermore.

Light out of darkness shall rise,
   Hope above all shining clear;
Daybreak is filling our eyes,
   Welcome the dawn of the year!

SISTER.

Sweet sister mine—for thee the day is done,
    And I must journey on ;
But spotless love and deathless memory
    Will go with me.

The days that knew us will arise again,
    In sunshine or in rain ;
We two from childhood never once apart—
    One mind, one heart.

We two that walked together side by side,
    Shall Death's dark hand divide ?
The heart will closer cling until we twain
    Are one again.

Alone ! with strangely altered sight I mark
    The sunlight and the dark,
So strange it all is now, that one might deem
    It is a dream.

The light that falls upon that mystic sea,

Is now enfolding thee ;

And waves of love encompass evermore

That silent shore.

A REVERIE.

THE past and present here unite,
        And are as one,
And in a fadeless mystic light
        Have dearer grown.
Again with beating heart I stand
Beside the brook, and hold a hand
        Within mine own.

The trees are casting shadows dim
        Across the way,
The birds have sung their farewell hymn
        To closing day :
The twilight creeps o'er hill and dell,
And still I whisper—" Fare thee well "—
        Yet lingering stay.

" The day is dead," the west wind sighs,
        The night grows old,
The stars look down like watchful eyes
        That secrets hold ;

But brighter stars reflected shine,
In eyes now beaming up to mine,
    From depths untold.

I only feel, I cannot tell,
    How dear thou art,
For words but mock the thoughts that swell
    My throbbing heart ;
But by thy tearful eyes, my sweet,
I swear that we, when next we meet,
    Shall never part.

And now, and now, our souls have met
    In one long kiss—
Two human hearts had never yet
    An hour like this ;
" Like this," a gentle voice replies,
" Look in our little darling's eyes,
And if no deeper feeling rise,"
    You look amiss.

A FRIEND OF THE POOR.

AFTER the heat of the day,
  Cometh the cool evening's close ;
After thy toil by the way,
  Peaceful, and calm, thy repose.

Tenderer heart never beat,
  Nobler voice never was heard,
Tears, or with laughter replete,
  Came every soul-stirring word.

Right in the heart of the city,
  Runneth a river of woe ;
Many with no one to pity,
  Sinks in the dark waters' flow.

Up through the air comes their weeping,
  Up to the cold midnight sky ;
But, in gold-getting and heaping,
  Hears not the city, their cry.

13

He with strong heart, and endeavour,
  Stemmed the deep waters alone ;
Saved from the dark flowing river,
  Many a perishing one.

Weep all ye poor, and distress'd,
  Orphans, all friendless and lone ;
He who hath gone to his rest,
  He made your sorrows his own.

What greater name can we give ?
  Name that will ever endure,
Long as sweet virtue shall live—
  He was the friend of the poor.

CHILDREN'S NEW YEAR HYMN.

WHAT, O New Year! art thou bringing?
　We now greet thee in our morn;
May not little children singing
　Welcome in the year now born,
　　　Let our voicing
　　　Be rejoicing,
　Welcome in the year now born.

Noon will come, and gentle even,
　Twilight in her sober grey;
Onward by the light of Heaven
　Till we reach the perfect day;
　　　Noon and twilight,
　　　Oh may Thy light
　Lead us to the perfect day.

Onward, onward, courage taking,
　He shall win who nobly strives;

Morning of the year is breaking,
Morning of our little lives ;
Courage taking,
Hope awaking,
He shall win who nobly strives.

Children we of mother Nature,
Little of her ways we know ;
We but love her every feature
As the seasons onward go ;
Changing ever,
Faithless never,
May our lives thus onward flow.

Lord we come from Thee, our Father,
Morn and noon will wax and wane,
When the night's dark shadows gather,
We shall go to Thee again ;
When, O Father !
Shadows gather,
We shall go to Thee again.

LOVE.

A SONG you ask ? what shall it be ?
  What can it be but Love ?
And lips and eyes give back replies,
  " What should it be but Love ? "

The one that gains your guileless heart,
  Ah, happy, happy he !
And tender sighs, from Love arise,
  " Yea ! happy, happy he ! "

But where can such a—He be found,
  With Hebe's self to pair ?
So hard a task, we well may ask,
  And echo answers—" where ? "

One lover sighs—" That happy man,
  Ah ! would that I were he,"
Another's cry—" By heaven, I
  Would drown him in the sea."

But what! oh, what would he not dare,
To spend and end his days—with
The Love that lies, in lips and eyes,
Of peerless Annie Naismith.

A NIGHT WATCH.

THE lurid sun had set,
Across the sky the black'ning rain-clouds swept,
And wildly surging met,
And over all the land thick darkness crept.

Like one that suffered pain,
The hollow moaning of the wind went by,
And then down came the rain,
Like tears to weary eyes grief-parchéd dry.

Throughout the whole night long
I heard the sobbing of the wind and rain,
That like a tale of wrong,
Kept ever beating in upon my brain.

" Is all our toil in vain ?
Is all the labour of the rolling years,
But adding pain to pain ?
And will the darkness end our hopes and fears ? "

" Our tearful eyes are blind,
But through the deep, deep darkness of the night,
　　At last !—Oh shall we find
The dawning of an everlasting light ? "

　　Deep silence fell on all ;
And then a whispering the trees among
　　That broke the night's dark thrall,
And hill and valley woke to joyous song.

　　Oh, welcome that glad voice !
Oh, welcome that bright glory stealing on !
　　Rejoice, oh, heart rejoice !
Behold ! behold ! the breaking of the dawn.

L. R. T.

Our best and greatest gifts we value most
  Not when in glad possession of the same,
But when we feel the good for ever lost,
  And vainly clasp a mem'ry and a name.

And so our town a sober aspect wears
  For one we've laid among the dead to-day,
Whose vanish'd life a faithful record bears,
  How great our loss in him who pass'd away.

We hear the streamlet's noisy babbling song,
  As o'er the linn its shallow waters leap ;
The great broad river voiceless rolls along
  To meet the waters of the mighty deep.

So thou, my friend, hast found the mighty deep,
  The everlasting mystery beyond ;
We walk in darkness, and in sorrow weep,
  Still clinging to the broken earthly bond.

A thousand years have come and pass'd away,

    A thousand years, and this is all we know ;

The great dark shadow meets us day by day ;

    There stood our friend, and there he lies full lo'

Deep vers'd in all the laws that regulate,

    And hold in sway the miracle of life,

What feelings filled thee when approaching fate

    Presaged to thy clear mind the final strife.

We followed thee, all through the changeful day,

    Till twilight shadows gathered into night,

And never turned our tearful eyes away,

    Till that deep darkness hid thee from our sight.

NEW YEAR.

1884.

MIDNIGHT hath pealed, and from the street
Is borne the din of hurrying feet.

"A good New Year!" the young man cries,
And hope is beaming in his eyes.

But old age smiles through gathering tears,
Ah me! how swiftly speed the years.

For as from hill top looking down,
The city dwindles to a town.

So from the hill top of the years,
Are narrowed all life's hopes and fears.

Old year what though we part from thee,
Hast thou not left us memory?

Sweet memory, blest heritage,
Where wander free the feet of age.

But hark ! that cry borne o'er the sea,
Of those who fight for liberty.

" Freedom ! " they cry, and at the word,
Fire, famine, pestilence, and sword.

Swift follow where the tyrant trod,
And all the land is red with blood.

The sky is louring overhead,
The earth is covered with her dead.

And furies in the battle lulls,
Leave every home a place of skulls.

" Peace and goodwill to all mankind ! "
A homeless echo on the wind.

With song and dance and kindly cheer,
We welcome in the new-born year.

Their music wakens deeper chords,
The roar of cannon, clash of swords.

Oh Christ of Nazareth ! are these
The fruits of eighteen centuries ?

VERSES.

From hopeful Spring to Winter snow,
   The budding and the flower time,
The seasons come, the seasons go,
   The sower's and the mower's time.
The season and the day comes round,
First saw thy leaf above the ground;
Come sun and shade, come wind and shower,
And make thy leaf a perfect flower.

   The music of the Christmas bells,
   With wind and wave in cadence swells,
The moonlight falls upon the sea,
    A river golden bright,
My thoughts like ships go out to thee,
    This peaceful night,
   And deeply laden ships are they
   With greetings glad to cheer thy way.

The year is growing old,
    And thou art far away,
But rolling river land and sea,
Will not divide my thought and thee,
    This Christmas day.
So I my gladdest greeting send
To one I love to call my friend.

A flower and a star, so runs the story,
    Beheld the other's glory,
And loved, and loved, but they so far were parted
    Died broken hearted.
A happier fate is yours to day
With love and unity alway.

The dewdrop and the flower's heart,
    Become of each a part,
The river rolling onward to the sea,
    A unity ;
The dewdrop and the flower, sea, and river,
May you as they be one, and one for ever.

VERSES.

HARK ! hark the bells ! a joyful sound,
It thrilled the flower hearts under ground.
The snowdrop whispered, " I with all my might,
    Am seeking for the light,"
" And I, the violet, the pioneer,
    Will soon appear,"
    Then fear not thou the darkness of the night,
    Work on brave heart, and meet the morning lig

A voice is on the stormy deep,
    And in the gentle breeze,
On mountain heights, 'neath heaven's lights
    And waving forest trees.
The voice is sad, the voice is glad,
    As glad or sad are we,
To you to-day—aye, and alway,
    A glad voice may it be.

The music of the Christmas bells,
Of many a happy meeting tells,
   And night—a night of stars that shine,
On lordly castles, humble cots,
Beyond compare, a garden fair,
   Of bright—Forget-me-nots,
Forget me not, oh friend of mine,
   My heart goes out to thee and thine.

14

FRATERNITY.

No anthem to the God of War,
  Nor love song to the fair ;
Our song shall be fraternity,
  The compass, plumb, and square ;
The mystic symbols brothers know,
  As only brothers can,
In word and deed, a noble creed—
  The brotherhood of man.

In love or war, where brothers are,
  A brother's heart-blood warms,
In love or war, he'll not be far
  When sounds the call—" To arms ! "
But gathered round the social board,
  A brother knows his plan,
To fashion fair, by plumb and square,
  The brotherhood of man.

Not level down, but level up,
   A brother's work shall be,
Then shall arise, before all eyes,
   The building—unity.
So by the symbols, brothers know,
   We end as we began ;
And higher hold than rank or gold,
   The brotherhood of man.

COMMUNINGS.

Awake to the glory of day,
  Oh! beautiful, beautiful Earth,
For even by death and decay
  Your wonders are brought into birth.

The earth, and the sea, and the sky
  Are full of glory divine ;
A gospel come down from on high,
  A true record, line upon line.

Ah! there are the pages revealed,
  Through no intermediate hand,
The mists of the ages concealed,
  Now heard like a voice through the land.

Our footsteps had wander'd afar,
  Away in the darkness of night,
With never the light of a star
  To break on our sad, longing sight.

We stood with pale lips on the shore,
   And saw the dark river sweep by,
Where deep silence broods ever more,
   And hush'd is the last weary cry.

And hearing that last weary cry,
   We stood, in the depths of our tears,
Despairingly questioning why?
   And compass'd by doubts and by fears.

Now clasping with hope to our breast,
   The thought that, whatever befall,
Obeys an eternal behest,
   The good everlasting of all.

THE NORTH JOURNEY.

Dedicated to Commercial Travellers.

ON business bent he left the Forth,
And journeyed to the stormy north,
The sky was clear, and calm the sea,
The happiest man on board was he.

Ah, short-lived joy ! a storm arose,
And rudely broke his sweet repose ;
Great heaving was upon the sea,
But greater heaving still had he.

The elemental war now waging,
Was nought to that within him raging,
An earthquake tore through all his system,
No ill that flesh is heir to missed him.

He cried—" Oh, I am sick alas ! "
And cursed the good ship Nicholas ;

If I am spared to end this journey,
Back here again I'll never turn me.

To Lerwick town on Sabbath morn,
More dead than living he was borne,
His hostess laid him in his bed,
And tied a wet cloth round his head.

There from the sorrow of the sea,
In blissful virgin sleep lay he,
His face assumed that aspect mild,
As when he slept—a little child.

He slept—but soon awoke in dread,
His trembling shook the very bed,
"What can that be, oh hostess tell?"
She answered—"Sir, it's just that bell."

He thereupon rose from his bed,
The lady from his presence fled,
Arrayed in white—all, all forgot,
But his revenge—this—this he wrote.

" Oh bell ! oh bell ! no words can tell,
How dreadful is thy clanging,
The wretch that swung thy rasping tongue
With thee should now be hanging.

On Sabbath day when good folk pray,
And hear thy hateful hammer,
I grieve to say that even they
Cry out—" that bell ! oh damn her ! "

Some say 'tis meant to represent,
Divines and elders wrangling,
And some would go to realms below,
Could they escape thy jangling.

Thou art alone the Devil's own,
Thy reign will be eternal,
He would not miss a sound that is
So utterly infernal."

He left in anger Thule's shore,
And crossed the North Sea nevermore.

BLASPHEMY.

" CRUCIFY Him ! " was the cry,
   " He hath blasphemed, let Him die ! "
Eager priests incite the multitude,
Then, as now, the church, the church's good,
   " Give Barabbas unto us,
   But the Nazarene our curse."
Robed in scarlet, crowned with thorns He stands,
" King ! " the rabble shout, and clasp their hands,
" King," you mocking cry—yea greater than,
Priest, or King, behold, behold a man !
   " Crucify Him ! " was the cry,
   " He hath blasphemed, let Him die ! "
Let Him die ?—you knew not in your strife,
You !—you gave the Galilean life.

   " Crucify Him ! " was the cry,
   " He hath blasphemed, let Him die ! "

Onward with that cry the church has trod,

Feet, and garments dyed with human blood,

    " Devotee of Faith give us

    But the Christ of thought our curse,"

Fearless Science daring to be free,

Fire and sword fulfilled the church decree.

Thought now leaves her to her own dark laws,

Truth has robbed her of her teeth and claws,

    No more agony of blood,

    Shall she give for love of God,

Learning from her victims if she can,

Higher, nobler faith, the Love of Man.

A SONG OF THE SEA.

Oh whaur is yer faeder da night, my bairns,
   Oh whaur is yer faeder da night?
Dere's a faersome roar on da sea and da shore,
   An' oh for da mornin' light.

I heard in a draem, oh when! oh when!*
   Da cry o' droonin' men,
An' weel I kent troo a' da noise,
   Yer faeder's voice.

He cam' in here, an' white wis he,
   An' weet as weet could be,
Thank God! thank God! I cried in my draem,
   Yer hame, yer hame.

    ·   ·   ·   ·   ·

---

* Alas! alas!

On leeward shore, 'mid breakers roar,
    That very hour was he ;
From wave swept deck, and crashing wreck,
    He plunged into the sea.

Vain hope in such unequal fight :
    But through the boiling foam,
Arose before his dying sight,
    Wife, little ones, and home.

THE END.

PRESS NOTICES.

" He dreamt he saw his northern skies,
  His pining heart grew strong,
And with glad tears within his eyes
  He wakened into song."

—L. J. N.

" Laurence James Nicolson is a native of Shetland, from whose storm-
beaten shores travels southward a race of men of active emotional nature,
bearing within them that northern fire which seeks an outlet in song or
vigorous movement.   To Mr. Nicolson is justly due the title of 'Bard of
Thule'—no verses we have met so thoroughly breathes as his of the atmosphere of the northern land, and skies made bright by the ' merry dancers,'
or reflect with such truth the charm of the island scenery and associations.

    .   .   .   .   .

" There is a note in Mr. Nicolson's song that must be recognised to know
him as he is.   Fatherland has been to him an inspiration, but the nervous
force of much of his verse also conveys the impression of a heart thrilling
under the enthusiasm of humanity.   In the production of his deeper moods
there is an ever-present sense of the mysteries of life and death, and a cheer-
ful reliance on truths of human nature—in short, a patient faith in science
and man, the expression of which gives to Mr. Nicolson a somewhat unique
position among our song writers.   In point of style his poems and lyrics are
noticeable for polish of diction, and an easy melodious flow, while they
evince command of varied metrical forms.   He has the selective instinct
which is not satisfied unless every word in a line adds to its music, and in a
special degree he possesses a poet's ear for rhythm and rhyme.   It is this
technical accuracy joined to other qualities of thought which, without doubt,
causes his songs to be so much in request with musicians.   Many of his
songs have been set to music, have been published in sheet form, and have
already become deservedly popular.   As a specimen of a pure lyric that
flows of itself to music, we give the following :—

' It was the time of roses,
    We met, my love and I ;
And Beauty's hand had crowned the land,
    And music filled the sky.
    Our souls were thrilled with rapture,
    I know not how or why,
We wandered on by mead and stream,
And love was life, and life a dream,
    Whate'er the spell
    I know full well,
    It was the time of roses
    We met, my love and I.

' But when the first pale snowdrop
    Was opening into flower,
My own ! my own ! was stricken down !
    But saved from wind and shower
    To keep my heart from breaking,
    One little bud for dower.
One little bud—a tender care
From my dead flower that was so fair,
    So I will trace
    A vanished face,
    When my own little snowdrop
    Is opening into flower.'

Nothing could well be daintier, more melodious, or effective as an expression
of enjoyment in love and life than the first verse, while in the second a note
of pathos is struck with touching power."—*Extract from Edwards' Scottish*

"DA LAST NOOST."

" 'Da Last Noost' is (I think) an unique production, but I devoutly pray it may not long remain so. I do not know of any other composition whose music and words are both by Hialtlanders; and these owning names so characteristic of the Old Rock as are the names of Laurence Nicolson and Thomas Manson. I cannot criticise this song. Its theme, its pathos, its associations, all touch me too closely to permit of my looking at it from any point but that of a Hialtlander in exile. I can only hope that native talent thus sweetly wedded will repeat itself, and that again and again there will be wafted from the Old Rock songs such as this to awaken in our hearts old memories, old ties, old dreams, old hopes. There has never been any lack of poetic talent among the natives of Shetland (or 'Hialtland,' as I ever love to call it), but our Isles have not produced many musicians, although the love of music amounts to a passion in our hearts, and most of our lads know how to wake the wild chords of the violin, with untaught, wonderful skill. Let us give thanks to Apollo for lending his lyre to Balder, and let us pray ever that the example of Mr. Manson may be speedily followed by other Hialtlanders. Laurence Nicolson's songs are eminently fitted for being set to music, and it is to be desired that his verses could be made more available by publication in book form."—JESSIE M. E. SAXBY *in Shetland Times.*

" 'Da Last Noost '—noost meaning the winter quarters of a Shetland boat—is a quaint and charming Shetland Folk Song, written by L. J. Nicolson and composed by T. Manson. Both words and music have a quiet simplicity and pathos, and many plain suggestions of the sea."—*Scotsman.*

"The pathetic song called 'Da Last Noost,' written by L. J. Nicolson, has been set to appropriate and plaintive music by Thomas Manson. The prevailing sadness of the piece demands that it should be cast in the minor mode, and the composer has succeeded in giving the mournful phrases an original turn, without interfering with the character of the song."—*People's Journal.*

"THE PRINCESS OF THULE."

" A pleasing task is assigned us in bringing to the notice of our readers the appearance of a song that honestly deserves a distinguished place in the repertory of all singers of cultivated taste in song music; and by those musicians, to whom the ephemeral prettiness of the modern ballad is but scant and enervating fare, the artistic and comprehensive beauty of 'The Princess of Thule' will be at once appreciated. The love of the young Princess for the land of her birth is told by Mr. Nicolson in lines whose poetic force and fire are very far removed from the insipidity of the conventional drawing-room song; and no higher praise can be given the composer than to say the music is worthy of these beautiful verses. Mr. Collisson displays much science and perception of effect in imparting to his charmingly fresh melody and accompaniment a local colour that is singularly appropriate to the weird grandeur of the 'lone land of the mist.' The song is a delightful one, and we cordially recommend it to all our singing friends. Two settings can be had. Keys G and E flat; compass, D to G sharp."—*Musical Star, Edinburgh.*

The Songs of Scotland. Chronologically

Arranged.   Edited by PETER ROSS.

EXTRACT FROM PREFACE TO THIRD EDITION.

IN compiling this work my design was to gather together a representative body of classical Scottish song with brief explanatory notes, and, where possible, with a few particulars concerning the lives of the writers. The chronological arrangement was adopted not merely on account of its novelty, but that the work might be illustrative of the successive stages of one branch—the richest—of Scottish literature. The various songs selected were printed as nearly as could be determined in the order in point of time in which they were written, the only exception being in the case of the Jacobite songs, which were arranged according to the events celebrated, so as to give, in a measure, a history of the Rebellion of 1715 and 1745 in verse. Much antiquarian and historical matter which could not be used in the body of the book was placed at the disposal of readers in the Introduction.

Another purpose was that the book should be thoroughly national. Nothing was admitted to its pages that was not the production of Scottish writers.

My idea was that the song minstrelsy of Scotland was in itself grand enough and varied enough to be measured by its native productions solely. This high standard was endorsed by many of the English reviews of the book, notably that of the London *Standard*, which closed a markedly appreciative notice by saying that the collection was " the most convenient and exhaustive we have seen of the songs of Scotland, which, taken as a body of lyric poetry, have not been surpassed even by the lyric poets of Greece, hitherto the supreme masters of the lyric muse." The same idea was also enunciated by the laudatory notice which appeared in the *Westminster Review*. Had the volume not been thoroughly Scotch, these compliments would not have been so clearly earned. In this connection, too, I cannot forbear quoting an extract from a letter by Professor Blackie on the national influence of our loved "hame sangs." "Next," he says, "to our Christian and independent pulpit, which we owe to John Knox, there is no moral influence to which Scotsmen owe more than to their Scottish song. It is not merely as a healthy recreation, but as a moral stimulant of the first kind, that Scottish song acts in forming the character of the Scottish people ; and in this respect, and also as being the best exposition of Scottish history, Scottish song ought always to form not only a prominent element but a pervading atmosphere in all Scottish schools. A familiar acquaintance with our rich treasure of national song is, in my opinion, far more valuable as a moral agent than the most exact knowledge of the principles of Greek and Latin grammar."

ALEXANDER GARDNER, PAISLEY AND LONDON,
Publisher to Her Majesty the Queen.